The
Fight
Back

J D Carter

First printing: 2016.
ISBN-13: 978-0-9572671-1-4

British Cataloguing Publication Data
A catalogue record of this book is available from
The British Library.

Also available on Kindle from Amazon

The
Fight Back

Books by JD Carter
The Party
The Fight Back

This book is for
the newest and the oldest members of my family.

First, for my little granddaughter, Ava.
She is so beautiful and she doesn't stop laughing.

And second to my mum Joyce and my dad Richie.
God bless them.

Chapter 1

Johnny Sabatini was freezing his nuts off. Forty minutes he had been waiting now and he was really getting pissed. He was going to give it another ten minutes, then he was leaving. He had been dubious about the meet all along. Alright, he had done some bits and pieces with these Serbs before but he didn't trust them one bit. The stuff he had been getting from them was good quality and the one they called Peter was okay, but he smiled too much for Johnny's liking; he was a bit over-friendly. The other one, he was a surly bastard and only ever spoke Serbian, so Johnny didn't know what the fuck he was saying anyway – but he was in charge alright. They were always asking him questions, like who ran things in the East End, whether they were part of a gang or working for themselves, could they shift a lot of gear, were they trustworthy?

But like Johnny told them, the East End had firms rather than gangs, and it was all down to who you knew – the people you grew up with and went to school with, or people from further afield if you had been in prison. But it also depended on which pubs and clubs you frequented. The only people who thought they were gangsters were the Jamaicans and the young Pakistani kids and Africans who were fighting each other for the lower end of the market.

Anyway, Johnny hadn't the faintest idea why the Serbs were asking him all these questions. He wasn't the brightest spark in the world and, like most lowlifes, he couldn't give a flying fuck anyway just as long as they kept giving him the gear to sell. That's all that mattered to him. That and the fact that he had enough spare stuff to shoot up into his arm and a few quid for the old woman to keep her quiet; that's all he cared about.

He took his phone out of his pocket and dialled the number they had given him. So what if he had been a bit slow in paying them their last bit of dough? He had most of it now and he was hoping they would let him have more gear to sell; her indoors needed some rent money.

He heard a crunch on the ice behind him. It was the last thing he would ever hear. The hand he saw briefly took hold of his chin and pulled it hard to one side, and then he felt the knife slide between the space in his ribs, straight into his heart. He was dead before he hit the floor.

His assailant knelt down at Johnny's side, took the phone from his hand and, searching through his pockets, took the money he was going to give them. Not bothering to look up at the Chrysler 3000 as it pulled up in front of him, the shadow-like figure got up, opened the door of the car and climbed in. The car pulled away slowly, leaving poor Johnny Sabatini lying on his back as his life blood flowed towards the gutter, turning to ice before it reached the kerb.

"Did you get his phone?" said a gravelled voice from the back seat of the car. Peter held up Johnny's phone between his thumb and forefinger and shook it. "Good," the voice said, as its owner settled back into his seat.

The Chrysler accelerated from the scene, turned the corner and disappeared into the night. Peter cleaned Johnny's blood from his knife with his handkerchief and folded it away for another day.

Chapter 2

Six months had passed since Bobby's death and Sharon had hardly given him a second thought. He was out of her life and good riddance – as far as she was concerned, the only two people who were ever going to worry about him were his Auntie May and her husband Ted. But poor old May had been struck down with a violent form of Alzheimer's disease, which was getting worse week by week, and Ted was struggling to cope with the situation he found himself in.

She went around every couple of weeks to see how Ted was coping; she felt it was the least she could do. But May didn't even recognise her; she thought Sharon was the little girl who used to live down the road from her when she was a child. When Ted asked her where Bobby was, she felt bad about having to lie to him, but she and Alex had made up a story that Bobby had left her, run off with a dolly bird and moved to Spain. When Ted heard this he just shook his head and said: "Sharon, love, if you do hear from Bobby could you please let him know that his Aunt May is ill and to get in touch."

"Course I will, Ted," Sharon had replied. "If I find out where he is, I promise I'll let him know that May is ill." She felt guilty saying this but she couldn't tell him the truth – that she had shot Bobby dead in a car park on his fiftieth birthday and that Alex and his friends had buried him in the foundations of the new building Charlie was constructing.

Sharon was just getting on with her life now and she only cared about two things: her son Alex, and her sister Ruth, who had started an affair with Michael Clay, otherwise known as 'The Angel of Death'. She told Ruth she was mad, warned her to watch out for that blue-eyed bastard; she didn't want her sister to get hurt but what could she do? Ruth was a big girl. Sharon would just have to be there for her if things didn't turn out the way she wanted them to. Sharon had one good thing happening around her and that was Poppy. God, that girl was good for Alex. It seemed like he had grown up overnight. He reminded her of his dad Clive more and more.

Chapter 3

Stevie Carter was waiting to make his move; he knew he was taking a gamble but fuck it, why not. Watching through a single lens Nokia night sight, he watched them unload their precious cargo. He guessed there was about a ton, maybe a little more.

Smiling to himself, he made the phone call to his friend, Liam who was waiting down the road with the transport. While waiting for Liam to answer he did a quick calculation in his head. "One ton of skunk at, say, £100 an ounce to get shot of it quick – that's £3,400,000. Bloody hell, that's not a bad night's work! Plus it's really going to piss that Vietnamese arsehole off, big time. Serves him right. No one mugs me off."

Little Ming, the Vietnamese arsehole in question, had, six months earlier, turned Stevie over for ten grand. Why, he couldn't figure out as they were doing good business. But that's what you got for trading with a greedy dog-eating gook. He could have waited one night and jumped out and stabbed him, or got hold of a gun and shot him, but no – this way was better as he knew it would really hurt Ming in his pocket; little Ming loved money more than anything in this world.

"Hello mate," he said into his phone. "Listen, he just put the baby to bed, so give it twenty minutes or so, alright." He paused. "What's that? Yeah, lovely, see you then." Having called Liam, he reached into the inside pocket of his jacket, pulled out a piece of paper and rang the number on it. "Alright? It's me, Stevie. Sorry it's so early but you did say to let you know as soon as ... Yeah, that's right, I got you that van you wanted. Good runner. Lovely condition. How does 3 or 4 sound to yer?" Having completed the coded message, he waited for the reply. "Nice one. See you this afternoon." He put his phone away, then rubbed his hands together. "Lovely jubbly."

Stevie watched as Ming's boys closed the shutters down and locked the side door. He couldn't help but smile as he turned over in his head the amount this little bit of work was going to net him. "£3,400,000!" he said to himself. "Fuck, that's a lot of dough. Take Liam's £25,000 off the top and that's still £3,375,000 all for little old Stevie. What a clever boy you turned out to be."

He knew Liam would be pleased with his whack as he thought they were just moving some gear for someone and twenty-five grand, that wasn't a bad payday for a couple of hours work by anyone's standards. This was the biggest bit of work Stevie had ever had; sure, he had dealt in quite large parcels before – forty, fifty kilos – but nothing this big. It was more than his wildest dreams.

Stevie and his buyer, Michael Clay, had known each other for years and Stevie knew he wasn't going to get turned over. He was getting £250,000 up front, which would cover Liam's bit of dosh and give Stevie a nice holiday somewhere; he hadn't made up his mind where yet but with that amount of money he could go anywhere he wanted.

He watched as the lorry pulled away and indicated to turn left out of the industrial park. Stevie waited five minutes then picked up his holdall and left his hiding place to walk the hundred yards to the lockup. When he reached the side entrance he laid down the bag. He knew there were no cameras to worry about; this was a run-down estate with cheap units for rent and no questions asked.

Stevie bent down and opened the holdall, took out a chainsaw and placed it on the floor. Taking hold of the toggle between his fingers, he tried to fire it up. On the fourth attempt, it burst into life, making a brrrrr, brrrrr, brrrrr sound as Stevie pressed the trigger, making the chain spin around furiously. Like something out of the Texas Chainsaw Massacre he attacked the door, cutting a large cat flap in it. There were no alarms; drug dealers didn't want the police snooping around if the alarms were to go off in the night by accident, so he didn't have to worry about that. He gave the cat flap a tap with his foot and it fell inside the unit. Stevie looked around as he dusted himself off. Everything was quiet except for the birds singing their dawn chorus.

Pushing the bag into the hole in the door he had just cut, he ducked down through it into the darkness. Taking a flashlight out of the bag and replacing the chainsaw, he searched for the light switch he knew was on the wall by the shutters. His hand was inches away from the switch when he changed his mind. He'd wait until he heard Liam pull up in the van.

Shining the beam of light around the warehouse, he searched for the boxes of skunk that belonged to Little Ming and found them stacked up in the middle of the floor. He walked over to them, placed his hand on one of the boxes and let his fingers glide over the edge as he walked the length of them. As the flashlight lit up the warehouse something against the back wall of the unit caught his eye. Walking over to it, he saw that something was hidden under a tarpaulin. He took hold of the edge of the canvas, threw it to one side and stared at the two large crates in front of him. One was about six feet long and two and a half feet square; the other was slightly smaller and had been left open, the lid not hammered back down properly.

Stevie tried to lift the lid off with one hand but it would not budge, so he put the torch down and tried with both hands. The lid creaked and groaned as the nails did their best not to give way but with one last effort it came loose. Stevie picked up the torch and shone it inside the crate.

"Shit!" He could not believe his eyes. "Well I'll be..." He laughed as he looked down at row upon row of hand guns. There must have been a hundred or more. All automatics, with spare magazines, and boxes and boxes of ammo. Knowing that he wouldn't be able to lift the crate by himself, he dragged it to the floor, the heavy thud as it landed breaking the silence and echoing around the warehouse. This was a real added bonus and Stevie couldn't wait to see what was in the other, bigger crate.

The lid was nailed shut so he shone the torch about him and saw a crowbar leaning against the wall about six feet away. Taking hold of it, he jammed it under the lid, using all his weight to push down. The lid gave a little, exposing a nail head. Putting the claw of the crowbar under the nail, he jemmied it up and it came creaking out of its hole. Stevie had to repeat this manoeuvre another nine times before he could lift the lid off the crate, but he wasn't disappointed. Ripping the greaseproof paper away, he was even more astonished at what he saw. Machine guns – Heckler & Koch 9mm, just like the Old Bill used.

"Happy bloody days!" he said out loud.

"Oi, Stevie, you prick!" Stevie was so engrossed in what he had found he hadn't noticed Liam banging on the shutters for him to open up. Quickly, he put the lid back on the crate and banged the nails back in as best as he could. He didn't want Liam to see what he had discovered. Satisfied that he had done enough, he jogged over to the shutter door, turned the power on, hit the big button and up they went.

"Where the fuck you been?" said Liam. "I've been stuck out here like a proper wally."

"Sorry, mate," Stevie replied. "I was having a piss out the back."

Liam pulled a face and tutted. "Well, where's the gear?"

"Over there." Stevie pointed to the middle of the warehouse floor. "Come on, let's not fuck about. Back the van right up so we can load it up as quick as we can."

"Alright, keep your hair on!" Liam did as he was told and backed the van right up on top of the boxes. It took them twenty minutes or so to load the van. Forty-five boxes, each weighing twenty-five kilos. Stevie was right: there was more than a tonne.

Liam jumped down from the back of the van and went to close it up, but Stevie called to him as walked away. "Come on, we ain't finished yet."

Liam looked puzzled. "Whatcha mean, ain't finished?"

"Just a couple of crates, but they're heavy bastards. So get back in the van and back it right up."

Liam cursed. "Fuckin' arsehole, you said it was only a couple of fuckin' boxes."

"Yeah, and now there's some fuckin' crates as well. Come on. The quicker you stop moaning, the quicker we'll be out of here."

"Wanker," said Liam, as he climbed back into the van and reversed to where Stevie was standing.

"Come on." Stevie pointed to the smaller crate. "Take the other side. We'll both lift this end on first, then lift and push together. Ready now? And go." They struggled but, working together, managed to get one end of the crate onto the back of the van.

"This ain't half heavy, Steve," Liam said.

"Yeah, I know. Come on, we can do it. Ready ... lift." Again they struggled but once they got the crate into the air they managed to push it onto the back of the van. "There. That weren't so bad, was it?"

The larger of the crates wasn't as bad as they anticipated. With the same amount of effort and a lot of grunting they got it in the back of the van as well. Closing up the back, they made their getaway.

As they pulled out of the warehouse Liam's curiosity got the better of him. "Well, come on then, what's in the bloody crates?"

Stevie smiled to himself. "Never you mind."

"What d'you mean, never fuckin' mind? I just broke my fuckin' back on them bastards!"

"Look, you've got twenty-five grand for half an hour's

work. Stop bitching and drive."

Liam glanced over at Stevie. "Yeah, and fuck you an' all."

Stevie took out a joint, lit it and had a couple of quick puffs before offering it to Liam. "Here, have this and stop moaning."

Taking the joint, Liam took a long pull on it. "I was only asking."

"Yeah, I know you was." There was a long silence. Then Stevie said, "Oi, you greedy sod, save us some." Taking the joint back from Liam, he inhaled deeply and started to think of all the things he was going to buy with his share of the money.

Chapter 4

Poppy made Alex wait a long time before she gave in and went out on a date with him. She had her reservations about their age difference as well as his reputation for violence and the way he earned a living. He had been honest with her and told her that was how he lived his life and he wasn't going to change it – not even for her.

But she already knew that because Charlie, Poppy's brother-in-law, had spoken at length to her about it. "The boy is what he is and there's nothing you can do to change him," he'd said, "but you will be able to rely on him to stand by you and he will love you because he's like his dad, and everyone thought the world of his dad – as does everyone think the best of young Alex."

She'd even had a word with Sharon, his mum, who told her she would be the best thing that could ever happen to Alex. Sharon had said: "You're a good girl and you'll be able to change him a little bit but don't expect miracles. He's a villain and always will be." She'd also mentioned that she had never known her Alex to talk about a girl the way he talked about Poppy and she knew he was in love with her. However, Sharon warned Poppy it was her life, her decision and they would still be friends no matter which way she chose to go.

Poppy thought long and hard about it. She knew she wanted a man in her life – but was Alex the right one? In the end she gave in. He had acted like a true gentleman towards her. He had only been late once and even then he had rung her and apologised. He hadn't tried to make love to her on the first date – he didn't even kiss her until their third date, and that was just a peck on the cheek. And when she asked him in for coffee he'd declined and said he wouldn't come in until she knew it was right and she was ready to give herself to him.

Poppy decided that if Alex wanted to play games they'd

play games, so she made him wait a little longer, until the right opportunity came along. They often played Michael Buble in the car and one day Alex told her he could get his hands on some tickets to see the singer in Paris. Would she like to go? Poppy said she'd love to see him and Alex suggested they fly there and back in the same day. Poppy looked him in the eye and said, "No, let's stay overnight." Smiling as Alex replied, "I hoped you would say that," Poppy put her arms around him and gave him a long, lingering kiss.

Chapter 5

Katie and her friend Michelle were walking arm in arm along Bethnal Green Road, laughing and sharing a cigarette. Katie was wearing a short tartan skirt with a chain and a padlock for a belt, Doc Martens and a t-shirt with a picture of the Sex Pistols on it. Her hair was tied in a bun with a metal tail comb holding it together, and she had heavy black make up around her eyes. Michelle wore a simple dark grey miniskirt, trainers and a plain white t-shirt that showed her belly. As they turned into Barnet Grove, Michelle noticed a Vauxhall Astra van had crept up behind them.

"Don't look behind you, Kate, but it's them fuckin' Pakis from the other day," she said.

Katie tried her best but couldn't help herself. Glancing back, she could see two boys of around 18 or 20 in the front seats of the van. In the back were another two boys, and they were all smiling at her.

"Hello, ladies. Fancy coming for a ride then?"

In unison, Katie and Michelle said, "Fuck off!" And kept walking.

"Don't be like that," one of the lads said. "We've got some good blow."

"Well get your friend to blow it up your arse then," said Katie, and they both started to giggle.

One of the boys in the back called out, "Think you're too good for us then? Think you're hard gangster bitches, uhh?"

"You fuckin' bet we are!" Katie yelled back. "Ain't no way you're getting near us. Besides, we don't go with Pakis, so piss off!"

The two guys in the back shouted: "Fuckin' bitches."

"Come on, man, let's get 'em," the skinniest of the guys said. "Who do they think they are? They're only white whores. Look at dem. Dey want it, man."

"Where we going to take dem?" the guy in the passenger seat asked.

"I know where, man. Just grab 'em!" cried the driver.

The van accelerated so they were in front of the girls. Then the back tailgate was thrown open and the two boys from the back jumped out and ran at Katie and Michelle, who were slow to react to the situation they found themselves in. The big thickset guy grabbed Michelle by the arm. As he dragged her towards the van he growled into her ear, "Come on, bitch. You're mine."

Michelle screamed, "Let go of me, you Paki bastard!" She hit out at him several times, bursting his lip. He slapped her hard with the back of his hand and, with the help of the guy who was in the passenger seat, pushed her, head first, into the back of the Astra.

Katie waited for the skinny one to get closer. "I'm going to fuck you and make you my bitch!" he taunted her. As soon as he was within striking distance of her foot, she let fly straight between his legs. He doubled over in agony and fell to the floor, clutching his groin. Katie ran and jumped onto the back of the thickset man. She tried to dig her nails into his eyes but the guy in the passenger seat grabbed hold of her hands and pulled her off his friend before punching her in the face. She fell to the ground. Before she could get to her feet, someone grabbed her arms and she was forced into the van. Her assailants climbed in after her, closed the tailgate and sat on her and Michelle. Katie felt helpless. Looking into her friend's eyes, she saw tears – and that's when she knew she had to stay strong for them both.

Skinny, clutching his bruised ego, had managed to get in the passenger side and close the door. Through gritted teeth he told the driver to get the fuck out of there in case they were seen.

***

The girls knew they hadn't gone far, but how far they had no idea. Katie guessed they were driven around for no more than 10 minutes before the van came to a halt. The driver got out and checked that all was clear before he banged on the side of the vehicle. The tailgate went up and the girls were pulled from the van. When Katie tried to protest, a dozen blows and kicks rained down on her as she was pulled inside the door of a house and led down a damp and dirty passageway. With wallpaper peeling off the walls and there was a strong smell of curry.

Every time she tried to turn around she got slapped or punched. It was dark, and difficult to see where she was going. Stairs appeared in front of her and she was forced down them. The guy she had kicked in the balls opened a door in front of them and she was shoved into a dingy basement room. She saw a couple of mattresses on the floor, a table, four chairs and a load of boxes stacked against the wall. She and Michelle huddled against each other in fear.

The four boys stood in the middle of the room, discussing something. Once or twice they looked over at the girls. Katie knew it was not going to be good. "I want the blonde one first," said the driver.

"Why you first, man?" asked the thickset one.

"Because I've got the gear to jack them up with and then we can play with dem whenever we like."

"Yeah, man," said Skinny. 'We turn dem into white junkie bitches and make some money out of dem. That's what my cousin does up in Sheffield; he's earned loads, man, out of dem young white girls up dere." Skinny was still holding his balls, but now through excitement at the prospect of raping Katie and Michelle – especially Katie for kicking him and embarrassing him in front of the others.

The men turned towards the girls and moved in closer, sickly grins on their faces. Michelle, not wanting to face her captors, buried her head in Katie's shoulder. Katie held tightly onto her friend and as they got closer she screamed at them, "Fuck off, leave us alone!"

But these boys didn't care what the girls wanted. They only had one thing on their minds: rape. Skinny and the passenger took hold of Michelle, pulled her away from Katie and pushed her towards the table. "Please, no!" she cried. "Don't! I'm only fourteen."

"I bet you're a virgin as well," said the driver, as he unzipped his trousers.

"I am. Honest! Please, please no!" Michelle cried out, struggling to get away.

"Oh man, I didn't think dere was such a thing as a white virgin," the driver said, laughing.

Katie went to move towards her friend but the thickset man shoved her back with the palm of his hand and said, "You're next, bitch – and I'm going to make you bleed."

Looking past the smirking thug in front of her to poor Michelle, Katie felt helpless. His words kept going over and over in her head. She watched as they pulled Michelle across the table, Skinny and the passenger holding her down by her arms. As she lay there on her back, screaming and kicking out at them, Driver pulled her legs apart and ripped her knickers from her body. Then, forcing her legs wider, he leant forward and spat between her thighs. "I hate dry pussy," he laughed. The others all laughed with him. He then commanded them to hold her down as he forced himself inside her. Michelle was crying as he grunted and thrusted away at her.

It was over in minutes. "Your turn, man," he said to Passenger, who started undoing his fly while Driver, still with his trousers around his ankles, took hold of Michelle's arms. As Passenger forced her legs into the air he noticed the blood on the inside of her thighs. "Fuck me, man!" he yelled. "Blood! She was telling the truth. She is a virgin."

Skinny giggled with anticipation. "Come on, hurry up. I want to have a go."

Katie couldn't watch her friend's suffering any more. She knew she had to do something and quick – or she would be next. Thickset had his back to her and was laughing at his friends enjoying themselves. Katie made her move. She pulled out the steel tail comb from her hair and plunged it into Thickset's neck with all the hate she had in her. He didn't even cry out. Three times she stabbed him, each time harder than the last. On the third time, he collapsed to the floor. She had hit his jugular. Blood pumped out of his neck onto the floor and ceiling as he tried in vain to stem the life blood flowing out of him.

Hearing the gurgling cry of anguish as their friend hit the floor with a thud, the other three stopped what they were doing. "Bitch!" Driver yelled, as he tried to pull up his trousers.

Katie didn't hang about. She ran for the door and managed to get it open before they could stop her. Running up the stairs two at a time, she slipped on the top one but kept going. Nothing was going to stop her from getting help for her friend. Running the length of the passageway, she flung the door open so hard it came back on her, but not enough to stop her. Not noticing the car turning the corner, she ran into the street as fast as she could.

Chapter 6

"Look out!" cried Alex.

"Fuck!" Tony swerved – but too late.

As the car hurtled towards the girl she tried to jump over it but landed on the windscreen, which collapsed inward with the impact. The car skidded to a halt, throwing her to the ground. Alex jumped out of the car immediately and rushed to her aid. As he turned her over he realised to his horror that he recognised her: it was the young girl who lived next door to his nan.

"Katie? Are you okay?"

Katie was dazed and confused. "Don't touch me!" she screamed into his face, as she tried to get away from him.

"Kate! Katie. It's me, Alex. You know me. I wouldn't hurt you, babe." Alex took hold of her firmly by the shoulders.

Katie froze for a moment. Then, recognising Alex, she suddenly felt safe. "No, not you. Them Paki bastards in there. They've got Michelle!" She pointed across the road.

"What?" Alex exclaimed.

"They raped her, and they were going to rape me, but I got out."

"What'd she say?" Tony appeared next to Alex.

"Something about some Pakis raping her and her friend."

Tony looked up just in time to see Skinny and Driver come running out of the doorway into the street. They stopped when they saw him and Alex at Katie's side. Tony didn't have to be told; their faces said it all. "Oi, you two!" he called to them. "Come here!"

Turning in panic, they fought each other to get back through the door. Tony stormed towards them in a rage, leaving Katie in Alex's care. As he reached the house he saw the two men disappear down the stairs towards another door. He followed right behind them but as he reached the bottom step he heard them lock the door. But that wasn't going to stop him. He started to walk towards the door. When he was a few paces away, a quick jump step and a side kick was all it took to make the door fly off its hinges. He walked through the door. Slowly, he looked around and saw poor Michelle lying on the table, with someone thrusting away inside her. Then he noticed a thickset man lying dead on the floor.

Driver came towards him, trying to intimidate him. "What you want, white boy?"

With a kick, Tony sent him flying across the floor and crashing into a pile of boxes against the wall. Skinny came rushing at him with a butterfly knife. Tony grabbed hold of his knife hand and threw a punch to his throat. Then, twisting his arm, he broke it over his knee. Skinny screamed in pain.

Passenger was trying to pull up his trousers as he pleaded. "Listen, man, I didn't want to do this. They made me!" He held his hand up in front of him as if to ward Tony off. Tony grabbed hold of his shirt, pulled him close and headbutted him three terrific blows. Then, picking Passenger up above his head, he slammed him down onto his back on the floor. Looking down at him, Tony felt nothing but anger for what these boys had done to two defenceless little girls.

Whimpering sobs of anguish and pain came from the prone Passenger. "Fuck you. Fuck you all!" Tony screamed. He jumped into the air and landed with both feet on Passenger's chest, breaking his ribs in several places. Tony stood there for a moment, not moving. "You fucking bastard!"

Hearing someone call, he turned. Driver was leaning against the door frame. "They were only fucking whores."

"No, they were little girls. And they didn't deserve that."

Driver, picking up the butterfly knife on the way, staggered towards Tony, who let him come to him. Driver lunged at him with the knife but Tony was like a whirlwind. Knocking the knife from his hand and hitting him more times than he could remember, he left Driver a mess on the floor.

Michelle was still lying on the table, crying softly to herself. "Sssshhh!" Tony said. "It's alright. They're not going to hurt you anymore." She tried to get up, but didn't have the strength. Tony took his jacket off, put it around her shoulders and helped her to stand. As she sobbed, he tried to comfort her. "Sssshhhh, sssshhh." It was all he could think to say. Michelle tried her best to stand but her legs were too weak. Tony knew she wouldn't be able to manage the stairs, so he picked her up and carried her up to the street above.

When Tony came out of the door with Michelle in his arms, Alex and Katie were leaning against the car. Katie tried to go to her friend's aid but she was in no fit state to walk herself. Alex held on to her, trying his best to keep her steady and stop her falling. "She's alright, Katie. She's with Tony. He won't let anyone hurt her ever again."

Michelle held her arms out to Katie, who fell into them as Tony gently let her slide to the ground.

"You alright, mate?" asked Alex. Tony nodded. "What about them?"

Tony followed Alex's eyes to the door. "Katie killed one of them."

"Good girl." Alex smiled. "And the others?"

"They're not dead, but I did my best."

"Well done, Tone. Well done."

Alex surveyed the scene around them and decided to call his brief. A small crowd was gathering and the police were no doubt on their way. People were on their phones taking photos. One lad walked right up to Katie and stuck his phone in front of her face, but Tony pushed him away and made him drop his phone to the floor. "Oi! Watch it, man," he shouted. Tony told him to fuck off or he would be needing an ambulance as well, and he backed off and melted into the crowd.

***

Sean Reilly, their brief, was a local boy turned good. He was one of the best young criminal lawyers in London but he had an advantage over his peers – his dad was a well know 'old face' and had helped his son understand both the Old Bill as well as the clients he would represent. Sean also had a younger brother, Alan, who was a brilliant accountant who could help you look after your money in many ways. Their father Billy made them work hard at school to get a good education, make something of themselves. He always said that no son of his would ever have to go across the pavement risking freedom and life to earn a living, and he was right. He'd made sure of that.

Sean told Alex to stay put as he was only five minutes away in Shoreditch having some lunch, and he was true to his word. Just as the ambulances arrived, so did Sean and the police.

The crowd was becoming hostile towards Alex and Tony, shouting insults. Rumours had started to spread about what had happened in the basement of the house across the road. More and more police were arriving to control the situation; the first ones to arrive knew that if they didn't get help quickly, it could soon turn into a riot.

The ambulance men started working on Michelle and Katie straight away. As they comforted the girls they worked carefully on Michelle's facial wounds, knowing they had to preserve the forensic evidence for a rape case to be proved. However, the looks on their faces told another story: they were more worried the poor little girl would go into shock.

The police pushed the crowd back to where they could do no more harm than shout in the name of Allah what they were going to do to Alex and Tony when they got their hands on them. Sean Reilly had managed to get to the front of the crowd and he called over to Alex, who asked the policeman to let him through. Ducking under the tape the police had set up to form a barrier around the crime scene, Sean led Alex away from the baying mob.

"Bloody hell, Al, this looks a bit naughty!"

"Yeah I know, but let's not worry about it for now," Alex said. As they walked, he quickly filled Sean in on what had happened in the last half hour.

They stopped when they reached the girls. Sean bent down on one knee and held out his hand as he spoke to Katie. "Hello. My name is Sean Reilly." Katie took his hand and shook it lightly. "With your permission, I would like to be your solicitor and take care of this terrible mess for you and your friend."

Alex crouched down next to them. "Katie, Sean is a good friend of ours and he will do right by you."

Katie stared warily at the scene surrounding her and started to cry. "I want my mum." The tears flowed freely down her cheeks as Sean cradled her in his arms, trying to comfort her.

"We have to contact their families, Al."

"Don't worry about that," said Alex. 'I'll ring my nan. She lives next door to Katie's family." He took his phone from his trouser pocket. "Hello? Nan? Yeah, I'm fine. Mum's okay as well. Nan... Nan, listen. I need you to go next door and tell Katie's mum that she's had a bit of an accident. Yeah, she's okay. I'm with her now. They are..." He put his hand over the phone. "Mate, what hospital you going to take the girls to?"

"Whitechapel," the ambulance man replied.

"Nan, they are taking them to Whitechapel." Alex paused. "What? Oh, sorry – I mean, Katie and her friend Michelle. Yeah, yeah. Look, Michelle is in a bad way so tell Katie's mum to get in touch with her parents and get them there right away." Moving the phone away from his ear, Alex raised an eyebrow at his nan's inquisition. "No. Tell them that her injuries are not life threatening but she's banged up a bit. Look, Nan, I've got to go. No, Nan, I'm alright. Will you stop asking me questions and just go and see Katie's mum? Bye... yeah, love you too. Bye, Nan." Alex put the phone away and scratched his head. "Talk about giving me ears a bashing!"

Sean smiled up at him. "So they are on their way then?"

"Yeah. Me nan's seeing to it now."

"Good."

Two detectives came pushing their way through the crowd. "Out of the way. Police officers," they called. The crowd reluctantly gave way and they climbed under the barrier tape. The taller one, who was overweight, introduced himself as DI Samson. He gestured to the younger copper, who was keeping the crowd at bay. "Sergeant Flood." He beckoned the young sergeant to come over. "Right, what do we have here then?"

"Two young white females. One's been raped; the other fought off the attackers with the help of these two gentlemen."

"Did the bastards get away then?" DI Samson asked.

"No, there's one dead."

"Fuck."

"And the other three are badly wounded. They're all in the basement of that house over there."

"Please tell me they are not Asian," the DI said, looking worried.

"Sorry," said the young copper.

"That's all we fucking need." DI Samson looked around at the scene before him. His gaze rested on Katie and Michelle. "They the girls?" Flood nodded. It was then that he noticed Sean, who waved to him. "What's he doing here?"

"Who?"

"Reilly."

Alex appeared from behind Sean and smiled at the detective inspector. "Oh fuck. This just ain't my day."

"Why's that?" asked Sergeant Flood.

"Why's that? I'll tell you why's that," DI Samson raged.

"Fucking psycho Alex Dicks is why's that!"

"And isn't that his shadow, Tony Woods, guv?" Flood said.

"Oh, it just gets better and better. I knew I should have called in sick this morning."

Sean walked over to DI Samson. "Hello, Peter," he said, holding out his hand.

"Fuck off, Reilly."

"Now, now. There's no need for that, is there, Peter?" Sean said, knowing his use of the DI's first name would annoy him.

"What are you doing here?"

"I'm here as I represent both Alex and Tony – and the young girls."

"Blimey. You didn't hang about, did you?" Samson exclaimed.

"Look, let's cut to the chase," said Sean. "I think we had better get the girls out of here and fast, as well as my clients, Alex and Tony." Samson went to say something but Sean stopped him. "Look, it could get nasty if we don't move quickly. There's a mosque down the road and they will be coming out real soon."

Samson looked to his sergeant. "He's right, guv," Flood said.

He ran his hand through his hair. "I suppose you're right," he said, looking puzzled.

"Look, what I suggest is that the girls go to hospital and the boys come to the station tomorrow and make their statements to you at about 12 o'clock. How does that sound?" Sean knew he had the DI by the bollocks.

DI Samson put his hands on his hips and sighed. "They're not going to run away? They just stumbled onto all of this?"

"12 o'clock," said Sean.

"They had better be there."

"They will."

The DI sighed again. "Go on. Get them out of here."

"Tomorrow then."

"You owe me one, Reilly," Samson called to Sean as he walked away. "And tell them they have to leave the car here for forensics."

Sean waved an acknowledgment as he walked back to the girls and Alex. "Right, leave the keys in the car and get out of here now. I will ring you later. I think I shall have to go with the girls to hospital as I need to protect them from DI Samson for a while. I'm sure the doctors will be on my side. I also have to get the girls' parents' permission so I can represent them."

"When do you want to meet us then?" asked Alex.

"Early. How about 9.30 tomorrow?"

"Okay. We'll see you then."

"And don't worry. I will sort this out, no problem."

Chapter 7

Ruth woke up at 8:30am and lay there in a half sleep, her eyes closed, as she remembered the dream she'd had earlier that morning. She and her sister Sharon were children, about eight or nine, feeding the ducks in Victoria Park. She remembered seeing people in rowing boats, teenagers splashing each other with their oars while at the side of the lake, dads were showing their sons how to bait a hook to try and catch a fish. Everything seemed idyllic until the man came and grabbed Sharon, put her under his arm and walked away with her. No one seemed to notice what had happened. Ruth stared after them, not knowing what to do. She tried to scream, "The man, the man!" but nothing came out of her mouth. Running to her mother, who was on a park bench talking to another lady, Ruth pulled at her dress and pointed to where the man was walking away with Sharon but her mum just told her to go away and play. She didn't even look at Ruth even though she was crying hysterically. Ruth turned to look in the direction the man was taking Sharon and, realising she was gone, fell to her knees, looked up at the sky and let out a piercing scream.

Opening her eyes with a start, Ruth sat on the edge of the bed and reached for the glass of water on the bedside cabinet, drinking it in two quick gulps. Then, gasping for air, she said, "Sod that!" and brushed the hair away from her face. Ruth hadn't dreamt in years. For some reason she turned and looked at the other side of the bed. Her husband Paul hadn't come home that night – not that she cared. He had been doing that a lot lately. Putting her hand to her mouth, she laughed at the thought that he was seeing someone else, someone younger. Not that it worried her. She was planning on leaving him anyway.

She heard a car pull up on the gravel outside her bedroom window and knew it was Paul's Aston Martin. The night before she was supposed to meet her lover, Michael, but he had rung and said something had come up and that he would be in touch in a couple of days. Ruth wasn't used to being told what to do or how things were to be. This was new to her. Paul was a walkover, as meek as a kitten. If she said roll over, he would; if she said jump, he would ask how high. God, it was a loveless marriage. Ruth had told Sharon that was why she had fallen for a bad boy: she wanted a real man and Michael was both real and bad. In fact, he was a very dangerous man, but she could not help herself. She was madly in love with him.

She heard the front door close, but no footsteps on the stairs. Paul must have gone straight to the kitchen. Ruth moved over to her dressing table and, sitting naked before the mirror, started to brush her hair. Smiling at her reflection, she watched as her breasts swayed to and fro to the rhythm of her brush strokes. She thought back to the previous night and how frustrated she had been that Michael wasn't at her side, making love to her. She started to explore her body with her hands, playing with her nipples the way Michael did, drawing her legs up and opening her thighs so she could touch herself. Wet with anticipation at what was to come, she pushed her fingers deeper inside her vagina, arching her back as wave after wave of pleasure rippled through her body as she climaxed, leaving her drained but very satisfied.

Putting on her dressing gown, she made her way downstairs to the kitchen. Paul, making coffee in a fancy Italian espresso machine, had his back to her. He called over his shoulder to her. "Want one?"

"Yes please." As Paul made the coffee in silence, Ruth sat down at the breakfast bar and stared at his back, her mind somewhere else.

Paul turned and placed her coffee in front of her. Then he sat down on a stool opposite her, rested his elbows on the counter, stirred his coffee and announced: "I've met someone else."

Ruth wasn't shocked or even angry, but the way he had just come out with it caught her by surprise. "What did you say?"

"I've found someone else."

Ruth couldn't believe her luck; she had been trying to think of a way to end their marriage for quite a while. She had even thought of asking Michael to murder Paul but dismissed the idea. She didn't hate him, she just didn't love him anymore; he had become so boring. "How long have you been seeing her?" she said, trying to sound shocked.

"A year. Perhaps a little longer." Paul was normally sheepish if he had done something wrong, but strangely, he sounded as if he didn't care.

"Do you love her?" Ruth asked.

"Yes, and I want to marry her," he blurted out.

Ruth took a sip of her coffee; she had to stop herself from laughing. Keeping the cup in front of her mouth, she asked, "So you want a divorce then, do you?"

"Yes please," Paul said. "I'm sorry. It just happened," he added, raising his voice.

"There's no need to shout, Paul! Let's try and discuss this amicably." Ruth was beginning to enjoy herself.

"I'm sorry." Paul got up and looked out of the kitchen window. Putting his hands on the worktop, he bowed his head and started to cry. "Ruth, things haven't been right between us for a long while, and she was just there for me."

"Who? Not that tubby little thing in the office!"

"Don't call her that – and her name, by the way, is Linda." The crying turned to heavy sobs. Paul's whole body shook as his crying got louder.

As Ruth watched him she began to feel sorry for him. She knew she hadn't been a good wife to him. She had used him, and in a way, she couldn't blame him for seeking love from someone else. Poor Paul. Rushing to his side, she put her arms around his waist and rested her head on his back. "It'll be alright," she said, "We'll work things out. Ssssshhh." Paul cried for a good eight or ten minutes while Ruth cuddled him and that was something she hadn't done in a long while. As his crying subsided, she rubbed his shoulder. "You feeling better now?"

Paul turned on the tap and washed his face with cold water. "Oh God." He sighed, Ruth handed him a clean tea towel and he dried his face. "Thank you," he said, wiping away the water. "You can file for divorce and cite me for adultery; I'll give you whatever you want. I won't fight it."

Ruth smiled at him. "Let's have a drink and we can talk this over because I don't know about you but I think I need one. Scotch?"

"Yes, please. Make it a large one, with ice."

"You can have whatever you like, Paul," Ruth said.

They sat down with their drinks and talked, which was something they hadn't done in years. Ruth didn't mention Michael, and Paul didn't tell her that Linda was pregnant. He said she could have the house and half of what he had, which was generous, but he would keep the flat in Butlers Wharf, that was only fair. They would sell the villa in Italy and spilt the proceeds between them. Paul told Ruth she would walk away with six and a half million and the house – which surprised her, as she didn't know he had that sort of money, but she was happy with the outcome.

He left that afternoon with most of his clothes and said he would come back for his records, CDs, books and of course his cars in a couple of weeks. Ruth helped him to his car with the bags, kissed him on the cheek and waved goodbye as he drove away. She stood there for a moment, watching the car disappear down the road, and then turned on her heels and rushed back indoors to phone her sister Sharon.

"Shal."

"Hello, sis. How are you?"

"I'm free as a fuckin' bird!"

"What?! What do you mean, free?" Sharon exclaimed.

"Paul. He just left me."

"You're joking!"

"No I bloody well ain't!"

"I don't believe it."

"I know. Great, isn't it?"

As she walked back into the kitchen to pour herself another drink, Ruth started to tell her sister everything that had happened that morning.

Chapter 8

Mark Clay was about to lock up the door that led to the office at the back of the Clay Brothers' warehouse and workshop. He had just put the key into the lock when he was shoved against the door and felt the cold chill of the barrel of a gun behind his ear. He knew there was nothing he could do.

A voice spoke into his ear. "Open up and let's go back up the stairs into your office."

The voice was foreign and Mark had no idea what its owner wanted. He could tell there was more than one person as he heard the shuffling of feet on the gravelled floor. He also knew he was fucked so he went along with whatever they wanted. He was marched up the stairs to his office door and forced to open it. Then he was thrown across the room. As he fell to the floor, he got a good look at the bastards. There were four of them, two with hand guns and one giant of a man brandishing a massive heavy duty stun gun. Their leader was smoking a cigarette between a very sinister smile.

They tied Mark to his office chair in the middle of the room. He tried to ask them what they wanted but all he got for his troubles was a hundred thousand volts shooting through his body. The pain was terrible and his body ached violently but he couldn't go anywhere as the gaffer tape they had used to restrain his arms and chest kept him from moving more than a couple of inches in his chair. The two men with the guns stood on either side of him, while Smiler sat on the edge of his desk, gave the giant instructions and smoked cigarette after cigarette as the night went on.

***

Michael found his brother the following morning after he had taken a phone call from Mark's wife asking where the bloody hell he was. Michael told her to calm down, that he would go looking for Mark. He just hoped he was behaving himself and not doing anything silly; Mark used to be a heavy gambler and had a real problem until Maxi made him go into rehab but he had been straight for a couple of years now – but you never knew.

Michael made a few phone calls. Nothing. He rang Mark's mobile. Same there – nothing. Ringing the office phone, all he got was a dead line, which was strange. Okay, he thought, let's start at the last place Mark was known to be.

As Michael pulled up outside warehouse he knew something was amiss, because the door leading to the office had been left ajar. He got out of his car, walked over to the open door and called up the stairs for his brother. No answer. Climbing the stairs two at a time, Michael paused at the top and listened. Nothing. As he reached for the doorknob he moved closer and glanced through the glass panel in the door. What he saw shocked him; he never expected anything like this. He thought Mark had gone on the piss or been playing poker all night but instead his brother was strapped to his office chair in the middle of the room, blooded and bruised, with a gag in his mouth. Michael could see pools of blood surrounding Mark's feet. Then he noticed the nails that had been shot into them to stop him from running away. As he went to open the door his brother's eyes stared wildly at him. Straining at his bonds, Mark shook his head in the direction of the door.

Normally Michael would have just rushed in to save his brother – but not this time. He opened the door a quarter of an inch. Mark was going mad, pointing with his eyes and head to the side of the door. Michael pressed his face to the glass and followed Mark's stare. Spotting the wire where there shouldn't be one, he closed the door quickly. "Fuck"" he said. He was lucky; he hadn't broken the contact.

He thought for a minute as he tried to come up with a way to save his brother. Then he remembered that the wall was only plasterboard on a metal stud frame. He could easily break through it. Looking around him, Michael saw a fire extinguisher hanging on the wall. That would have to do; it was heavy and he could smash his way into the office in no time. Taking it off its wall mount, Michael began hitting the wall on the other side of the door, away from the wire. It took no time at all before he had made a hole big enough for him to stick his head through. "Hold on, Mark!" he shouted. "I won't be long. I'll get you out of there!"

Another three or four whacks with the fire extinguisher and there was enough room for him to force his way into the office. He had to break pieces of the wall away with his hands as he got stuck halfway through. Michael was covered in dust but he had no time to worry about that; he had to reach Mark, who was getting weaker by the minute. Stumbling as he finally made it, he reached out to his brother and pulled the gag off him. "Hell, Mark, what happened?"

Mark gasped for air. "Michael ... water. Get me some water!"

Michael went to the small kitchenette area, grabbed the first thing he saw, a big old pint glass, and filled it to the top. Hurrying back to Mark, he held the glass to his mouth. Mark drank slowly at first, then started to gulp at the water and began to choke.

"Steady," said Michael. "Now who done this to you?"

Mark tried to answer him but his throat and mouth were still dry from the gag being forced into his mouth and his words were barely audible. "Fuckin' Eastern Europeans."

"What?! Serbs?"

"How do I know? They all look the fuckin' same to me. Greasy hair and leather jackets." Mark started to cough.

"Here, drink some more – but slowly this time."

"Mike – the bastards tied me up and shot nails in me feet so I couldn't get away. It di'n' half hurt!"

Michael cut his brother free from the tape that was

holding him bound to the chair. Kneeling down to look at the nails that held Mark's feet to the floor, he felt the blood seep into his trousers. Anger welled up inside him. He looked up at Mark. "I don't know what to do, bruv. I don't want to cause you any more pain."

"Fuck the pain, just get me out of here!" Tears ran down Mark's cheeks. "I don't suppose it will hurt any more than what I've already been through," he said through gritted teeth.

Michael put his finger on top of the nail and tried to wiggle it free. It didn't move. Then he gripped it with his thumb and index finger and pulled.

Mark cried out. "Aaaahhh!"

Michael jumped and let go of the nail. "I'm sorry, mate, but I think I had better call Maxi." Not waiting for a reply, he took his phone from his pocket and rang his older brother. "Maxi, it's Michael. I've found Mark in his office and he's in a bad way."

"What do you mean, you've found Mark in a bad way? What, he's pissed?"

"No, no, I mean a bad way. He needs a doctor right now. Those fuckin' Serbs have tortured him and nailed him to the fuckin' floor! I think he's going into shock. I don't know how long he is going to last. Please hurry up," Michael said.

"Keep him warm, Mike, and try and get something hot inside him." Maxi's brain went into overdrive. "I'll be there as soon as I can."

"Alright Max, quick as you can mate." Michael knew his brother didn't hear his last words as the phone had already gone dead. Turning to Mark, he tried to comfort him. "Listen, Maxi's on his way and he is bringing help, alright, so you hang in there, okay." Mark's head was resting on his chest. He tried to talk but it came out as gibberish; he seemed to be flitting in and out of consciousness.

To Michael, it seemed like forever waiting for help to

come. He made his brother some sweet warm tea and forced Mark to drink it. He also dismantled the bomb, which was a crude device, but capable of blowing the office – and Michael and Mark – to pieces. He wanted to hug his brother and tell him everything was going to be alright but Mark was so covered with bruises he knew he couldn't. Michael felt so helpless. So he just kept talking to Mark instead. He talked about when they were kids, all sorts of shit, just to keep him awake. He didn't want his brother to fall into a coma.

Michael could see the burn marks where they had used the stun gun. They were everywhere; Mark's neck, face and body were covered. He could even see that they had pulled his tongue out and stung him there as well. Michael started to cry. "Mark, I promise you I will not stop until I've personally killed every one of them bastards. Boy, am I going to make them suffer for what they've done to my baby brother!"

He wiped away the tears when he heard the cars pull up outside the office. Looking out of the window, he was glad to see that Maxi had brought Bob with him. Bob was an ex-army surgeon who was now a vet, but he stitched up the odd villain or two every now and then just to keep his hand in.

Michael shook his brother gently. "Everything's going to be alright. Maxi's got old Bob with him. He'll have you right as rain in no time."

Michael waited at the top of the stairs to greet them. Maxi had brought the O'Brian brothers, Stevie and Tony, with him – and just in case the Serbs came back, they were both heavily armed. Maxi had a very worried look on his face as he climbed the stairs. "How is he, Mike?"

"Not good, Max. He's in a bad way."

"Come on, let's let old Bob have a look at him." Maxi led Michael back into the office, where he stopped dead in his tracks. "Oh my God!"

Bob squeezed past him and put his bag on the floor next

to Mark. He smiled at him. "Well, I must say you look a sorry sight, but don't worry, old Bob's here to look after you. We'll fix you up in no time." Despite his reassuring words, Bob knew he had to get to work on Mark straight away; he was going into shock and Bob needed to get some fluids into his body quickly. He opened his bag and, seeing that Maxi was still trying to take in the situation before him, called Michael over. "Here, hold this up high, will you?" he said, handing Michael a saline drip. Michael did as he was told and held the drip high in the air while the doctor inserted a catheter tube needle into Mark's arm. "There now, let's get you out of this mess, shall we? Max," he said, calling over his shoulder, "we are going to need some kind of jig saw to cut the floorboards. I need to lie Mark down before I can work on these bloody nails."

Maxi snapped out of his trance and held his hand to his head. "Err, yeah. There must be something like that in the workshop downstairs. Hold on, I'll have a look." He walked to the outer office and disappeared down the back stairs that led to the workshop.

"What do you think, Doc?" said Michael.

"He'll live. His wounds look worse than they are. As for the nails in his feet, they look nasty and must be painful but they are not life-threatening. He's lost some blood but nothing to worry about. It's the shock to his system that has me worried. We must keep him warm."

Maxi came back into the room holding a jig saw, a circular saw, a claw hammer, a pair of pliers and some mole grips. "Will these do, Doc?"

"Jig saw," said the doctor, holding out his hand like the surgeon he used to be. He put the saw blade into the gap in the floorboards and pressed the trigger but nothing happened. "Max," he called. "Plug it in, would you, please."

"Sorry," said Max. He looked around for a plug socket.

"Under the desk. I can see an extension lead." Bob

pointed with his free hand.

Max pulled the lead from under the desk and plugged in the saw. "Ready, Doc."

Bob fired up the jig saw and began to cut through the floorboards around Mark's feet. Fortunately, none of the boards were nailed into the joists and they all came away easily. By now Mark had no idea what was going on around him; he just sat there with his head slumped on his chest. "Right, that's it," Bob said as he shut off the jig saw and gently lifted Mark's feet, the boards still stuck to them. He looked up at Michael and Max. "I need you both to help me get Mark up onto the kitchen counter. Mark, listen to me. We are going to lift you onto the counter. Is that alright?"

Mark's eyes were closed but he was still conscious. "Just get them fuckin' nails out, will you, Doc? Please. They really hurt."

"That's exactly what we are going to do. Just hold on a little while longer." The doctor stood up and put his arms around Mark's chest. "Michael, Max – take hold of a leg each, would you? And Mike, keep those fluids up high as you can. Ready – one, two, three and lift together."

Pain shot through Mark's body as they lifted him up and moved him to the counter top. "Ohhh, sweet Jesus! Ohhh fuck!" He opened his eyes and looked at Maxi. "Make them bastards pay, Max. Please make them fuckin' suffer."

"I promise you, Mark, they will." Tears welled up in Maxi's eyes as he watched his little brother in such pain.

The O'Brian brothers looked over their shoulders when they heard Mark call out, but what could they do? Bob was the only one who could help Mark. However, they did know they would be called on at some point because this was war and Max was going to go all out on this one. Nothing was going to get in their way until they found the bastards who had done this to Mark.

As they placed him on the counter, Max saw Mark's head roll to one side and his body go limp. "Oh fuck! Doc, tell me he's not dead!" Maxi pleaded.

Bob felt Mark's pulse. "He's alright. He's fainted with the pain, that's all."

"Thank Christ for that," said Max.

The fact that Mark fainted was a bonus. Quickly, the doctor placed the mole grips on the nail on Mark's left foot and told Max to hold on to the piece of floorboard tightly. Pulling with all his strength, he gave it a couple of twists and the nail came free. He let the nail drop to the floor. "Right Max, now the other one." Holding the mole grips again, he gave a sharp twist and the second nail came out easily. "There, got the blighters," Bob said. He dropped the nail and began to inspect the wounds more closely before cleaning them.

Michael and Maxi felt helpless as they stood there watching the doctor work on their brother. Bob injected something into Mark's wounds and then started to bandage his feet. There was no need for stitches; the wounds were only holes, which would heal up by themselves in time. "Max, what do you want to do with Mark?" he asked.

Maxi answered without looking at the doctor. His eyes were for Mark only. "I want to find whoever done this to my little brother and kill them."

Bob smiled. "That's not what I meant. I mean, do you want him to go to hospital?"

"Not if we can help it, Bob. Don't really want other people sniffing about. Is there any chance we could keep this quiet?"

"I don't see why not. I can keep an eye on him. I'll visit every day at first, then as he gets better I can see him once a week. It's going to take time – at least four months before he'll be walking again."

Maxi looked at Michael, who shrugged his shoulders. "At least he's alive."

Maxi thought for a moment. "Okay, Bob. We'll take him home. Will you come with us and explain to his wife the sort of nursing he is going to need?"

"No problem."

"Thanks, Bob. And don't worry – we will look after you."

"Oh, I know you will," said Bob, with a large grin on his face.

Chapter 9

Tony was in Pellicci's cafe in Bethnal Green Road, waiting for his breakfast. He was also waiting for Alex, who was running a little bit late, which was unusual for him. He noticed a couple of schoolkids in uniform in the corner. They were mucking about and were told by the owner in no uncertain terms to stop it or they would get a thick ear. That made him smile, as he remembered he and Alex being told the very same thing many years ago.

He wondered if the schoolboys were going to be future young turks, the way it was for him and Alex. Tony often wondered, if they were straight, would they still earn the money that they did now? For a start they would have to pay a lot more tax, which he didn't like the idea of. At the moment they were down as company directors of a haulage firm that one of their friends owned, which they also had a small interest in. It also covered them with the authorities, as proof that that was how they earned a living. He thought long and hard about it for all of a couple of minutes but he always came to the same conclusion, which was that he liked things as they were – so fuck it.

He was just about to wipe the plate clean with a slice of bread when his phone began to ring. "Hello?"

"Tone. Just had a call from an old friend of ours. So get your skates on. I'll be outside in five."

"Just finished. See you in a mo," Tony said. He knew not to ask questions. Placing the bread back on his plate, he took a last mouthful of tea and stood up. "Money's under the cup, mate," he called to the café owner as he left.

***

Stevie Carter was in the travel agent's when he got the phone call; he was just booking himself a nice holiday in Barbados. The screen of his phone said number withheld, but he answered it anyway. "Hello? Michael, how are things going with you? Good, I hope." Stevie didn't like the sound of the voice on the other end. Standing up, he walked away from the travel assistant's desk. She threw him a concerned look, as if to say 'Don't cancel on me, not after all this hard work.' Putting his hand over the mouthpiece, Stevie said, "Sorry but I must take this call." He walked over to the corner of the shop by the front door so no one would overhear.

"Is everything okay?" he asked into the phone. He had a bad feeling about what he was about to hear, and he leant against the wall for support. "Something's come up and you can't help me out," he repeated back into the phone. "Listen, Mike, I can hold on a couple of days if that's any help to you. But I won't be able to hold on too long, you understand." Stevie grimaced into the phone. "Oh, you do understand, and that's why you're pulling out so I can find another buyer. Well, thanks very much!"

Stevie couldn't believe what he was being told. He moved the phone away from his mouth. "No, no!" he said to himself. "Not another fuck up, please. Not again." Feeling tense, he screwed his eyes up and brought the phone back to his ear. "Mike ... Mike, no I'm not getting stroppy. I just don't understand, that's all. I thought we had a deal." He looked out of the window into the street. Everything was a blur: the cars, the people. It was like he was watching his big payday, his big chance, floating down the drain. "I'm sorry," he said, then kicked himself. Why was he apologising to Michael? "Another time maybe?"

The reply came slowly. "I don't think there will be another time for me."

Stevie's heart sank. "Yeah. Okay." Slowly, he took the phone from his mouth and ended the call. Looking out of the window again, hands on hips, he said, "Fuck. Bollocks!" He almost had tears in his eyes.

Then he saw it in an old, closed-down video shop: a poster for a film from a couple of years back. American Psycho. "Alex!" Stevie said out loud. Grabbing the door handle and opening the door, he called back to the assistant, "Catch you later on, love, alright," and disappeared down the street.

"I fucking knew he was a time waster," the shop assistant said to her work colleague as she threw the documents she had just printed into the waste paper basket.

Chapter 10

Alex was quite surprised to hear that Stevie Carter was leaving messages for him all over the place, for they hadn't seen each other for at least a couple of years. At school, he had been part of their clique and they had shared some good times together, but they weren't close friends, more acquaintances. However, after a phone call or two a meet had been arranged.

"He's late," said Tony.

"Give him a chance. He could be stuck in traffic or something. And besides, he's only five minutes behind schedule," Alex said. Tony sighed heavily. He always thought Stevie was a bit of a prick, a ladies' man who liked to boast about his conquests and what he had done to the said young ladies the night before. "You got somewhere else to go then?" Alex said.

Tony fidgeted in his seat. "No," he said, none too convincingly. The leather of the car seat creaked under his weight. He hated people who were late and he was getting bored. He started to drum his fingers on the window.

"For fuck's sake, Tone, what's the matter?"

Tony sat in silence for a few seconds before blurting out, "It's just…"

"It's just what?"

"It's just that I've got an important date later – with Joanne."

"What do you mean, important?" Alex turned round and put his arm behind Tony's headrest. "What's so fuckin' important then?"

Tony looked embarrassed. "It's our anniversary."

"It's what?"

"You heard. Our anniversary. It's six months we've been together."

Alex laughed. "Do me a favour! 'It's our anniversary!'" he

said, mockingly. He laughed again. "Fuck me! And I thought I had it bad."

Tony was just about to seize the moment, try and switch it round and take the piss out of Alex, when a BMW pulled up alongside them. Alex pushed the button to wind down the window, as did the driver of the beamer.

"Hello Al. Tone."

"Alright Steve. What's this all about then?" said Alex.

"I think I've got something you may be very interested in."

"And what might that be then?"

Stevie smiled. "I've got a couple of crates full of machine guns and hand guns, and some nice hand grenades as well."

Alex and Tony looked at each other in surprise before smiling back at Stevie. "You bet we are," Alex shot back.

"Well, if you gents follow me I'll take you to the little beauties."

"Is it far?" Tony asked. Alex gave him a dirty look. "Joanne!" he said.

"Fuck Joanne," Alex replied. He turned to Stevie.

"Not far at all. Fifteen minutes, tops."

"See," Alex said to Tony. "Won't take long. About an hour or so, okay?"

"Sorry Al. Yeah, that's plenty of time," Tony said.

"Oh, by the way," Stevie said, almost as an afterthought, 'could you boys handle a ton or so of skunk? Only my contact's let me down."

"Fuck me, he's come up in the world!" Alex exclaimed as he started his engine. "Lead the way, Stevie boy!"

Stevie turned his car around and they slid in behind him in the traffic. He'd been right about one thing anyway; it didn't take long, and soon they were pulling into a small industrial estate off the Kingsland High Road in Hackney.

Alex pulled up alongside Stevie's car and Tony went to

get out when Alex said, "Glove box." Tony opened it up and took out two pairs of calfskin gloves that they always carried, just in case; you never knew what you were going to handle from one day to the next. He handed Alex a pair and they got out of the car.

Stevie already had his hands around a big old lump of a padlock and was turning the key to open it. Then he bent down and opened another one on the bottom of the door, and a third at the top. "There you go, all done," he said. Then, taking hold of the handle, he gave the door a shove with his shoulder. They followed him inside. Stevie fumbled for the switch and, one by one, a row of fluorescent lights lit up the space before them.

Walking past the boxes, which were piled high in the middle of the room, he waved his hand and said, "There's your skunk. And over here we have…" Stevie disappeared into a side room and it took Alex and Tony a couple of seconds to catch up with him. When they did, he was standing in front of the large crates he had told them about. "My little beauties," he said, holding his hands out to the side, like a priest taking mass in front of the altar.

Alex and Tony stood there a few seconds before Alex said, "You can stop posing now, Steve, and show us what you've got."

Stevie lowered his arms and lifted one end of the lid. "Give us a hand, will you, Al?" He pointed to the other end of the crate. "Only it's a bastard to get off." Alex put his gloves on and took hold of the crate lid. Together, with a great deal of straining and effort, they managed to prise the top off. "There you go. Help yourself." Stevie gestured with his free hand.

Tony reached in and pulled out a Heckler and Koch machine gun. He held it up and cocked it. "Brand new. Very nice indeed."

"Everything there is nine millimetre, including the hand guns, which are all automatics. There's two types: Glocks and another make, Sig." Stevie was grinning from ear to ear.

Alex moved over to the other crate, opened it and picked up one of the Sigs. Turning it in his hand, he asked: "How much ammo?"

"There's five thousand rounds, but I've been in contact with an old friend of mine and he said he can get another eight thousand for you." Stevie joined Alex and picked up one of the Glocks. "Each gun has two spare magazines and the Kochs have three each. They're thirty round magazines for the machine guns and fifteen for the hand guns. That's a lot of fire power."

"I've heard of Glocks, but where do Sigs come from? Don't want no Eastern Bloc shit," Tony said.

Before Stevie could answer, Alex spoke. "They're Swiss. Used to be standard issue for the CIA or FBI, if I remember rightly, and the Glocks are Austrian. So they're top notch." Alex fondled the Sig, feeling the balance and admiring the workmanship.

"Special Forces all over the world use Heckler and Kochs, as well as our Old Bill, so you know you've got the best." Stevie was doing his salesman act but there was no need; Alex and Tony were sold.

"So how much you looking for?" Alex said, putting back the Sig and taking the machine gun from Tony. Reaching into his pocket and pulling out his phone to use as a calculator, Stevie started to punch in some numbers.

"Where did you get them from, Steve? Only I didn't know you were into gun running," asked Tony.

Stevie scratched his head a few times, paused, then answered. "Tell you the truth, they were a bonus." He checked himself, and then asked, "You have anything to do with Little Ming?"

"Can't stand the bastard. Coming over here and nicking all our trade," Alex replied.

"Thank fuck for that, because that's where I got this lot.

It was with the skunk so I took the lot."

"What? So you're telling us that you nicked this lot off of Little Ming?"

"Serves the cunt right! He should never have turned me over for a lousy few grand."

That's when Alex smelt a bargain. He now knew he had Stevie by the bollocks: he had lost his buyer and he couldn't put this lot on the open market without Ming getting a sniff of it and coming after him. "So how much skunk you got and what do you want for it?" he asked.

"Err, let me see. There's eleven hundred and twenty-five kilos at a hundred pounds an ounce. I make that three million eight hundred and twenty, seven thousand and five hundred pounds."

Alex chuckled. "You're having a laugh, ain't cha, Steve?"

"No, Al. That's what it comes to at a hundred an ounce."

"But we're not buying ounces, are we, Steve? We're buying kilos. How are we going to make a profit at that price?"

Stevie looked puzzled; he had hoped to find a buyer at the price he wanted. "How much you want to pay then?"

"Well, nowhere near that! We were thinking more like fifty an ounce," Tony said.

"Fifty? Fuck off! You're taking the piss now."

"That's a lot of money to come up with at short notice, and we don't sell on street corners to justify that kind of money an ounce," Alex said. That knocked the wind out of Stevie's sail. "Who else are you going to go to? Because that's four people who already know you nicked Ming's gear, and it won't take long for word to get about and Ming will be on your tail in no time. And from what I've heard, those two little bitches of his love to cause a bit of pain on his enemies."

Stevie had heard the stories and he knew Alex was right. He couldn't keep offering the skunk all over the place without Ming hearing about it. He punched in the numbers, and stared at his phone. It was still a lot of money and he had the guns to sell as well. "Okay, that's still over one point nine mill for the gear."

"And what do you want for the guns?" Alex said with a smile.

"Twenty-four MPS threes at fifteen hundred a piece, that's thirty-six thousand for them." As Stevie hit the buttons on his phone's calculator his smile grew bigger and bigger. "Hundred and twenty handguns at, say, five hundred, that's sixty grand. And the extra eight thousand rounds of ammo at fifty pee each, another four grand. And I'll tell you what – you can have the other five thousand rounds for nothing. Oh, and there's the dozen hand grenades and various smoke and stun grenades, you might as well have them an' all."

"That's very nice of you, Steve," said Alex. "So how much does that lot come to altogether?"

"Let's see." Stevie punched in the last number. "Not bad!" he said out loud. "One hundred thousand, six hundred pounds. Plus the skunk, that's two million and fourteen thousand, six hundred pounds you boys owe me."

Alex looked at Tony, who sighed. He turned back to Stevie. "Do you mind if we have a chat?"

"No, go ahead."

Alex and Tony moved about five yards away, keeping their voices down Tony spoke first. "What you reckon then?"

Alex put his arm around Tony's shoulder and grinned. "Fuck him." Tony laughed. He looked over at Stevie and smiled. Stevie, looking like he had just won the lottery, smiled back. "Just go along with me, Tone," Alex said. Tony nodded. He didn't know what was going to happen next, but he had a feeling Stevie wasn't going to get what he was expecting.

Alex turned to face Stevie. "This is how I see it," he said, as he walked back to where Stevie stood. "You've nicked this lot, right?"

"Yeah." Stevie's expression changed; he didn't like the way Alex said that.

"Therefore you're asking us to take stolen property."

"So?"

"Well, you know stolen goods don't fetch nothing like their wholesale value."

"Leave it out!" Stevie choked.

"Listen, you stole this lot off a very nasty fucker call Little Ming."

"Yeah. So what?"

"And you've already tried to sell it to someone else who turned you down."

Stevie was getting frustrated now. "Look, Al, what are you going on about? This is fuckin' good stuff!"

Alex cut him off. "Hear me out." Stevie got a bad feeling that things just weren't going to go his way. "I bet Little Ming is doing his bollocks right now, wrecking his brains out about who would have the audacity to steal this lot off him. Now already someone else knows you have his gear, and that's a weakness."

"Michael would never grass me."

Alex didn't have a clue who Michael was, but it didn't really matter; he was only using him as a wedge to get a better deal. "That's a lot of gear you have here and I bet you don't know that many people who could handle it, and that's why you came to me. Isn't it?" Stevie sat down on one of the crates and looked up at Alex. "Listen, Steve. The more people you go to, the more you're making yourself unsafe. Ming will have his eyes and ears everywhere waiting for you to make that mistake."

Stevie hung his head and looked at the floor. He was worried now, and Alex could see he had nowhere to turn. "Now hear me out here, alright? We are prepared to give you one point eight million and that's the only offer you are going to get from us."

"You're taking the piss! No. Fuck it, I'll take my chances. That's crap!" Stevie exclaimed.

"No it's not," said Tony. "We'll give you £250,000 up front and the rest in a month."

"Nar. Fuck that for a game of soldiers. I've said I'll take my chances."

"You're living on cloud nine, mate!" Tony said. "Who do you know who's got two mill in cash? Because I'll be fucked if I know anyone who has. And if they tell you otherwise they are fuckin' lying, because all they want to do is get their hands on your gear and fuck you over for the lot." Stevie was looking more and more desperate. He stood up and ran his hand through his hair, not knowing how to answer Tony.

"Look," Alex said, 'so you go elsewhere. You break it down into smaller parcels – which takes time that you haven't got, because the longer you hang about, the more chance old Ming will find you."

"Fuck," said Stevie, pacing up and down in front of them.

"Who's your partner?"

"Ain't got one."

"Someone must have helped you! Because there's no way you shifted this lot by yourself. And what I would want to know is can he be trusted?" Alex gave a little chuckle.

Stevie's eyes narrowed as he went deep in thought. "Look," said Tony, "we're handling large amounts of blow all the time. We can send half of this lot up north, and the other half we can distribute between half a dozen different contacts. No one will even look at us twice. And as for the guns – what you going to do, start selling them to street gangs and Peckham gangsters? For fuck's sake, Steve, you'd definitely have that little Asian arsehole after ya in no time at all."

"Fuck it, fuck fuck double fuckin' fuck!" Stevie shouted, kicking the side of one of the crates. "This morning everything seemed fuckin' hunky dory." He brushed the hair out of his eyes. "And now…" He threw his hands up and turned away from them.

Alex knew he had him. "Steve, go with us, mate, and there'll be no aggro. As we said, we will give you quarter of a mill up front. You can pay off your bod and fuck off out of the country."

Tony pulled Alex towards him and whispered in his ear. Stevie heard Alex say: "Yeah, I'm cool with that… Listen, Steve, Tony's just come up with an idea."

Stevie let out a sigh. "Go on, let's hear it."

"Why don't you go to our place in Cyprus? It's a lovely villa. You can wait out there and we'll have your money sent over to ya. Or if you want to come back and get it yourself it's up to you."

It was like a light bulb going off in Stevie's head. "You can do that?"

"Hang on," Tony said. "I don't think that's a good idea, Al."

"Why's that?" Alex said, turning towards Tony.

"Well, I just think he would be safer if he stayed out of the country and we set an account up for him so he can get access to it from anywhere in the world. Of course, a small fee would have to be charged for that though."

Stevie smiled. "I don't like the idea of a small fee. I think that's something you two should sort out. But I do like the bit about the bank account."

Alex held his hand out to Stevie. "Done!"

Stevie shook Alex's hand and then Tony's. "Do you boys mind if I keep one of them guns? Only I think I'm going to have to get rid of my weak link."

Alex shrugged his shoulders. "Help yourself."

Stevie reached in and took out one of the Glocks and a box of ammo. "Come on, let's go. You can pick this lot up tomorrow."

As they walked out of the lock up, Alex and Tony decided they had a lot more respect for Stevie. He was taking care of business.

Chapter 11

Randall was cleaning his car outside his house, a nice three-storey townhouse overlooking Victoria Park in Bethnal Green. It was a nice quiet street but very up-and-coming and arty-farty, with lots of trendy people moving into the area who worked in advertising and the theatre and had kids called Christian and Abigail. He was just finishing off after giving the car a good coat of wax when he heard his wife Maureen scream out loud and call his name. He turned to see her standing at the top of the steps that led to their front door with the phone in her hand and tears streaming down her face.

"Maur!" he called to her as he rushed to her side, nearly tripping over the jet wash that he had just used on the car. His wife collapsed into his arms, sobbing and crying. "What's the matter?" he asked, puzzled and concerned.

"It's Leon! The bastards have stabbed him!" she cried into his face.

"Where is he? Is he alive?"

"I don't know!"

Randall took the phone from his wife. It was dead so he hit the redial button. The name Kieran – Leon's friend – came up. "Kieran, it's me, Randall – Leon's dad. What's happened?"

"They stabbed him, Randall!"

"Who? Who stabbed him?"

"The fuckin' Somalians, man! Five of them. He didn't stand a chance."

"Where is he?" Randall asked.

"In the market square in Bethnal Green Road."

Randall jumped the steps and got into his car. He heard his name called out; it was his youngest child, Rachel, who was only twelve. He spun the car round, wound down the window and called to her, "Look after your mum," before pulling away, burning rubber as he went.

He was only five minutes from the scene of his son's attack and, on seeing the crowd in front of him, he mounted the pavement, driving straight at them. He pulled up only inches away, making some of them jump out of the way and curse him. But he didn't care. His only thought was his son. Pushing his way through the crowd, he saw Leon's girlfriend Latisha cradling him in her arms, crying and stroking his face. Randall took hold of his son's hand.

"Leon, it's me, Dad. Can you hear me?" There was no response. "Son, it's Dad. Please talk to me."

Leon's eyes fluttered but they didn't open. "Dad," a murmur came. A tear trickled down his check. "It hurts! Oh Dad, it don't half hurt." He tried to move and the pain ripped through him. "Aaahhh!"

In the distance, Randall could hear the two-tone wail of the ambulance. "Everything's alright, help's on its way, Leon." He gave a nervous chuckle, believing in the chance that a miracle could happen. Looking into the crowd, he saw his son's friend Kieran, who smiled and nodded back to him. Whoop, whoop. The ambulance arrived. "They're here, son, you'll be alright," Randall said. But his smile slowly disappeared as he felt the life drain out of Leon's body.

He heard the ambulance man say, "Make way please." Leon's hand went limp in his. Latisha screamed his name and fainted at his side. As the ambulance man knelt down beside Randall, he said: "Excuse me, sir, we'll take care of him now."

Randall replied, "You're too late. He's gone."

The crew man looked for a pulse. He shook his head and told his crew mate to take care of Latisha. Randall reached for his son, took him in his arms and started rocking him back and forth. He kissed the boy on his forehead and told him he was sorry for not being there for him. The crowd stood silent in respect of a father in his anguish at not being able to protect his son.

More sirens sounded. It was the police, turning up late as usual.

***

Randall didn't remember much more about that night. There was lots of crying and screaming from his daughter and wife; family members came round to try and comfort them. But it was all a haze to him.

He walked outside for some peace and fresh air. As he leaned against the door frame, he put his hands into his pockets and felt something. He pulled out a phone. Leon's phone. He didn't even remember picking it up. He touched the screen, opened it up to the phone menu and pressed Kieran's number. It rang a couple of times before Kieran answered.

"Who's this? Who the fuck's got my bruv's phone?"

"Cool down, Kieran. It's me – Randall."

"Oh. Sorry, Mr Hopkins. I didn't…"

"It's alright. Listen, can you talk?"

"Yes, Mr Hopkins."

Randall smiled for the first time that night. "You don't have to call me Mr Hopkins. My name's Randall."

"Err, okay. Sorry, Randall," Kieran said.

"I'm going to ask you something and I want you to answer yes or no. Do you understand?"

"Yes Mr Hop… Randall."

"Good. Now do you know who killed my son?"

"Yeah," came the reply.

"Then I would like to meet you," Randall said.

"When?"

"How about now?"

"Where?"

"Outside York Hall Baths, in about ten minutes."

"No problem. I'm on my way."

"And Kieran?"

"Yeah?"

"This is just between you and me."

"Sweet," Kieran said.

Randall put Leon's phone away, took out his own and rang a different number.

"Randall, that you?"

"Yeah, it's me."

"Oh mate, I'm so sorry."

"Thank you, Alex," Randall said. He paused. "I need a favour."

"Name it, Randall. You name it."

"Can I call on you tomorrow?"

"Course you can," Alex replied. "I'm at your beck and call."

"Thank you."

"Anything you need?" Alex asked.

"That's why I'm calling. This could get heavy." Randall sighed.

"I don't care if it weighs a fuckin' ton, mate. Me and Tony are there for you."

"Thank you, Al. I'll call on you later."

Closing the phone, Randall walked down the steps to his car. He could still hear his wife's cries in the background.

Chapter 12

Little Ming was going crazy in his office, which was at the back of one of his many gambling dens, situated behind one of his many nail bars in the East End. "Who got my guns?" he shouted at the top of his voice to those gathered around the table. No one would look him in the eye; they all stared at the floor, too frightened to look at their boss. "Who got my skunk? You tell me! No one steal off Ming!" Taking a revolver from the waistband of his trousers and placing it under the chin of the first man on his right, he grabbed hold of his hair and, pulling it violently to one side, said: "Ho, you steal my guns, my skunk?"

Sweat started to pour down Ho's brow and run into his eyes. He looked for help but none came. Instead, he pleaded for his life. "Boss, please. Me no steal from you."

Ming screamed in his face, "You lie!"

"No, boss, no. You been good to my family, I know."

Those were his last words, for Ming had gripped the revolver so hard his finger tensed on the trigger. The gun went off, splattering Ming's face with Ho's blood as his head exploded all over the table. Young Choe, who had been sitting next to Ho, was showered with his friend's brain and flesh. Shocked by what their boss had just done, the five men and two young girls, Thi Kim and Thi Le, were too afraid to say anything.

When Ming let go of Ho's hair and the young man fell to the floor, he looked almost as shocked as them. He placed the gun down on the table in front of him. Taking out a handkerchief, he wiped the blood from his face and hands and spoke softly to them. "See what you make me do. I no want to hurt Ho. I want to hurt arseholes who steal from us. I want to know who knew about guns, who got my skunk." He looked at them long and hard. "Don't let me find out it one of you." He pointed his finger around the table. "If I find out one of you did this dishonourable thing to me..." He paused for effect. "I kill whole family." The girls looked to each other, then back at Ming. "Go." He waved them away with the back of his hand.

As they left the table, amid scraping of chairs, he looked at Choe. "You stay." Ming looked down at Ho. "Choe, you must get rid of body and clear up mess." Choe just nodded. Ming picked up his gun. Then, turning away from Choe, he tucked his revolver back into his waistband and walked away.

Chapter 13

Pete got off the train at Liverpool Street station. It had taken him just under four hours to get there from Marbella and now he was sitting in a cab. Another twenty minutes and he would be home. He was glad he was coming home; he had got the terrible phone call the night before from his dad. His younger brother Leon had been stabbed to death – and he was gutted. Alright, Leon could be a wind up and a pest, but he was his kid brother and Pete should have been there to look after him. But at the back of his mind he knew he couldn't have done anything. They ran in different circles: Pete was four years older than his brother and a right tearaway, whereas Leon was a gifted musician and footballer who trained over at the Arsenal. He'd been going places.

Pete's dad Randall had sent him over to Spain to work for a friend of his, as Pete was getting into a lot of trouble and the police were beginning to take an interest in him. So Randall stepped in and sent him away – but now he was back, and if he had his way it would be for good.

He looked out of the window of the cab and felt the tears start to roll down his cheeks. In his head was an image of his brother running away from him, laughing, after knocking the Sun newspaper out of his hand, and him chasing Leon and knowing he would never catch his younger brother as he was a far superior athlete and better runner than Pete would ever be. He searched in his pockets for a tissue but found none.

The cab driver must have noticed this, for he opened the divide in the window and said, "'Ere, son, want one of these?" He held out a small box of paper hankies.

Pete leant forward and took a couple. "Thanks," he said, as he wiped away the tears.

"You okay?" the driver asked.

"Yeah, I'm okay."

"You don't look it."

"Don't I? Well." Pete paused and took a deep breath. "I lost my little brother. He was murdered yesterday as he was coming home from school."

The cabbie's expression said it all. Closing his eyes for a brief second, he shook his head. "I'm so sorry, son. I really am."

"That's okay. It's just that..." The tears started to flow again.

"Go on, boy, let it all out. It will do you good."

Pete clenched his fist as he looked away from the cabbie. "I'm the fucker of the family. It should have been me, not him!" He hit himself in the chest with his fist. "Me. Not my little bruv. Me." His voice rose in anguish. "He was the quiet one. I'm the fuckin' arsehole. Aaaaahhh!" He swallowed hard and tried to choke back the tears.

They rode in silence the rest of the way, Pete letting out a sniff now and then. As they approached Bonner Street to turn off towards Pete's house they noticed all the flowers in the market square, and people young and old standing in prayer or quietly paying their respects to a life lost so young. The cabbie went to say, "Is that the place?" but before he could finish, Pete said, "Yes, it is." As the cab turned off Bethnal Green Road, Pete looked back at the crowd and felt touched.

A couple of minutes more and he was home. The cabbie didn't have to ask which house was his; the tributes said it for him. Flowers were everywhere. As the cab came to a halt, Pete moved to the edge of his seat and asked the driver how much he owed him. But the cabbie wouldn't have any of it and refused the fare. Instead, he offered his condolences to the family. True EastEnders were like that. Pete tried to protest but the driver told him, "Go on, get out. Your family need ya."

"Thank you." Pete stepped out of the cab but as he went to walk away the cab driver call out to him.

"Son!" He paused. "Be careful."

Pete gave a little smile. "Why do you say that?"

The driver leant out of his window. "Revenge is sweet, but even sweeter when the bastards don't know where it's coming from. So don't make your move too soon, alright?" He winked and pulled away.

His words made Pete chuckle, but he also knew they made sense. He looked around at the flowers outside his home. Most had messages saying how sad it was for a young man to die in his prime when he had so much to look forward to. He hadn't noticed that the front door was open. There, standing in the doorway at the top of the stairs, was his dad, Randall.

"Hello, son."

Pete climbed the stairs. "Dad. How's it been?"

"Not good. Not good at all." Randall nodded. "Come in, your mum's waiting for you."

As Pete walked past his dad he glanced up at him. "I'm not looking forward to this one bit."

"I know, son, but best get it over with." He pulled Pete close and kissed him on the top of his head.

Hearing the sobs coming from the front room, Pete found his mum clutching a photo of Leon. He put down his bag, sat next to her on the arm of the chair and put his arm around her shoulders, cuddling her tightly. As he felt her pain as a mother, he swore there and then to take revenge for his brother's death.

Chapter 14

Sergei Dmitri sipped his coffee from a very expensive coffee cup, his little finger sticking out into the air. On the finger was a ring with a diamond that was far too large and sparked like a ballroom glitterball, but Dmitri didn't care. To him it was all about showing how powerful he was, from his clothes to his cars and the beautiful woman on his arm.

He looked out of the penthouse suite he had just acquired on the Southbank and admired the London skyline. Olga, his young wife, who was twenty-five years his junior, stood at his side, her arm around his waist. He liked what he saw and he wanted to own it all. He was ex-KGB and since the fall of the Berlin Wall he had become one of the most powerful crime figures in Eastern Europe. Now he had decided he wanted to add London to his conquests.

"This will all be mine," Dmitri said. Olga looked up at him and smiled. She placed her hand on his shoulder and stroked his neck gently with the tips of her fingers. "I promise this. I will give London a year, maybe two – but no more."

"All of it?" Olga said.

"But of course, all of it. They are weak; they are not organised like us. We will crush them like little bugs, one by one." Dmitri smirked. "Petrov, what were their names again?"

Petrov, who was sitting in a leather armchair, looked at the Russian mafia crime boss's back. "The Krays and the Richardsons."

"Yes, yes, the Krays and the Richardsons." Dmitri finished his coffee, throwing his head back as he swallowed the last drop. "They were the last ones to have control in London. They only had fifty percent between them, but I shall have all control."

Chapter 15

Michael had dunked his biscuit in his tea just a little while too long. Lifting it towards his mouth, he saw it start to change shape and begin to buckle and droop. He tried to get it in his mouth quickly but too late – it broke in half. He just managed to catch it in his hand before it fell into his lap. "Shit."

"What's that?" said Mark, coming out of his pain-induced catnap.

"Nothing. Biscuit broke."

"Oh."

Michael got up and walked to the kitchen to wipe his hands, but not before licking the remains of the biscuit from his fingers. Turning the tap on and washing his hands clean, he dried them on a tea towel he found on the worktop. As he came back into the room he heard Mark say something. "What you say, Mark?"

"They broke me, Mike."

Michael looked at his brother sternly. "How do you mean, they broke you?"

"The Serbs, the fuckin' Eastern Europeans, whoever they were. They broke me." Mark started to cry.

Michael hadn't seen his brother cry like this since he was a kid. "Come on, Mark, there's no need for this." He pulled the coffee table close so he could sit facing his brother.

"No, Mike, you don't understand," Mark said, gripping his brother's arm. "I talked."

"What do you mean, you talked?"

"I told them about us – about everyone." Mark's body started to tremble and his hands were shaking so badly they were banging against his leg, making a slapping sound.

Michael was taken aback. He didn't know what use the information Mark had given them would be, or how much damage he had done. He realised he had to talk to Maxi – who wouldn't be pleased one bit. But first he needed to know more about what Mark, under the influence of torture, had told the Serbs. Looking at Mark that moment, lying there on the couch, he didn't recognise him as his younger brother. Mark had lost a lot of weight and he was drawn and thin. The bruises were still visible, and he was having terrible nightmares and sleeping poorly. Walking was still causing him a lot of pain and the Doc said he wouldn't be able to walk properly for a couple more months. The bastards were going to pay big time for what they had done. But first...

"Mark, I need to know what happened that night. What you told them."

At first Mark was silent. Then, taking a few deep breaths, he started to speak. "I didn't see them coming. I had my mind on other things; I was late as it was. Lorrie had just rung me and given me a bollocking for being late. She said dinner was in the oven so I was in quite a rush. The first I knew they were there was when I felt the barrels of their guns on either side of me neck when I was locking up. They made me open up again and led me back into the office, where they taped my arms to the chair in the middle of the room. The smarmy one who done all the talking took a nail gun out of a sports bag. I'd hardly got the words 'What the fuck do you want?' out of my mouth when the bastard shot a nail right into me right foot and pinned me to the floor. I let out a scream and he put one in my other foot and I screamed even louder. You could say at that point I knew I weren't going nowhere. I asked him what he wanted because if it was money they were after there wasn't none kept on the premises. That's when the horrible cunt with the fag in his hand said something in a foreign language and they all set about me. Three of them bashing the daylights out of me with their fists and stamping on the nails in me feet. Then one of them hit me with a chair over my head and I passed out." Mark lowered his eyes. Then, with venom in his voice, he asked, "And guess what they used to wake me up with."

"I don't know. Tell me," Michael said.

"Stun guns."

"Stun guns?"

"Yeah, fuckin' stun guns and I tell you something for nothing, they don't 'alf hurt. They hit me all over my body, how many times I couldn't tell ya. They just kept poking me with them over and over. The smarmy one was smiling all the time and the one with the fag in his mouth, his expression never changed, fuckin' blank it was. Then for some reason he just held up his hand and they stopped. Then he walked over and stood in front of me, took another cigarette out of his packet and lit it with his dog end."

Michael was getting more and more wound up with every detail that Mark told him.

"And then the bastard put out his butt on my forehead. I heard the hiss as it hit the sweat on my brow. Then I felt the burn and I cried out again but he just turned away from me and told them to beat me again. By the time they had finished both my eyes were closed, my body was a mass of bruises and I was black and blue all over. I could smell his cigarette but I couldn't see him – but he was there, giving the orders all right, telling the smarmy one what to do and what questions to ask."

"What did they want to know?" Michael asked.

"They asked about our slot machine business, how many we had and where they were, you know, what pubs and clubs they were in." Mark took a mouthful of his tea; it was lukewarm. "That's horrible! Get us a glass of water   please, Mike."

Michael went to the kitchen and searched around until he found a pint glass. He filled it up with water and ice and took it back to his brother to quench his thirst. "There you go. Nice and cold."

"Thanks, Mike." Mark took a long drink from the glass

before continuing. "They must have learned their trade in the Bosnian war because I tell you something, they were bloody good at it. I told them we were just businessmen and that I didn't know what more I could tell them. But they weren't having any of it. Stoneface said something to Smiler, who stood about two foot in front of me, stretched out his hand and put the stun gun straight on me nuts. I yelled no! But it didn't work; he held it there for a good ten to fifteen seconds. I felt as if I was in the electric chair in some godforsaken prison in the deep south of America where no one gave a shit. Only these boys weren't trying to kill me; they just wanted to hurt me good and proper."

By now Michael had a weird look in his eyes as he swore revenge on all and sundry. "What else did you tell them?"

"They asked about money lending."

"We don't really get involved in that, Mark – and anyway, Maxi takes care of that side of the business. Even then it's only to people we really know."

"I know, Mike, but they were on a fishing trip trying to find out anything they could about us. I don't think they know a lot, and that's why they were giving me the third degree." He drank some more water and crunched one of the ice cubes. He was also getting uncomfortable where he had laid in the same position for so long so he shifted his bum and propped his pillow up to ease the pain. "They asked about who the top dog was and who has the most firepower. I told them bits and pieces, you know, enough to keep them satisfied. I know something though."

"What's that?"

"Some of our enemies will be put upon before our friends." Michael laughed along with his brother. It was the first time he had seen Mark do that since he was hurt. Mark's mood changed back quickly to things at hand when he said, "Mike, there was one thing that troubled me."

"What's that then?"

"They kept asking me, who was Alex? On and on they went on about him. Saying Psycho Alex, how many men work for him, what does he do, how many girls does he control?"

"Alex ain't got no girls working for him. That's not his game."

"I know that and you know it too, but they don't. Quite honestly I don't think they know a lot about anything," Mark said.

Michael got up and started to pace the floor. "That's all these Eastern Europeans think about, is drugs and the sex trade."

"Yeah – for now," said Mark, 'but once they have a foot in the door it will be too late. There'll be no stopping them."

Michael took his phone out of his pocket. "I'm calling Maxi," he said.

"I tried to hold out, Mike, honest," Mark pleaded with his brother. "Only I don't remember everything I might have told them and that's what's frightening me." Tears entered his eyes as he looked up.

Seeing the look on his brother's face, Michael told him not to worry, that he would sort it out.

"Hello Max. It's me, Michael." He looked down at his younger brother. "I think we have a problem."

Chapter 16

Stevie wasn't looking forward to topping his old friend, but Liam was his weak link and no matter how he tried to justify keeping him alive, he kept coming back to the fact that he was an arsehole and he had to go. Especially after he bumped into his cousin Paulie Cook, who told him that he had just seen Liam in the betting shop boasting that he had a right few quid coming his way in a couple of days. And when Paulie asked him how come, Liam put his finger to his lips and whispered that he had just turned some mug over for all his gear. But he was so coked up and pissed the whole betting shop heard every word he said.

Stevie made out to laugh and say what an idiot Liam was. Then he made his excuses and told his cousin they would have to get together for a drink sometime. He got into his car and made a beeline for the betting shop but by the time he got there he was too late. As he rounded the corner he saw Liam being dragged across the pavement and thrown into the back of a car by Little Ming's cronies. Thi Kim and Thi Le were barking orders to Ming's thugs and when someone from the betting shop tried to intervene, Thi Kim spun round and back-heeled him, sending him crashing back through the betting shop's glass door.

Stevie cursed and banged his fist on the steering wheel. "Keep calm, Stevie boy, think," he said to himself. But he knew there was nothing he could do. Taking out his phone, he rang Alex.

"Hello Al. Is there any chance you could let me go to your villa a bit sooner rather than later?" A smile appeared on his face. "Thanks mate. Yeah, tomorrow will be fine. Could you let me have a bit of dosh? Only I need to do a bit of shopping. Aaah, thanks again, I appreciate it. See you round the Vic at midday then."

Stevie had no family except for a couple of cousins and –
as from today – an ex-girlfriend so it would be easy for him to
vanish into thin air. No one would even bother to try and find
him. Except for Little Ming – and he wasn't going to hang about
for that. He was off to start a new life for himself.

Chapter 17

"What the fuck's going on?"

"Shut fuck up, curly boy," said Thi Le.

Liam was sitting in the back of a Mitsubishi Evo with Thi Le on one side of him and Thi Kim on the other. "Come on, girls. What's it all about?"

Thi Kim hit him on the side of his chin with the back of her hand.

"Aaah! What's that for? I only asked a fuckin' question!"

Thi Kim hit him again, only this time with the back of a clenched fist.

"You fuckin' bitch!" Liam grabbed her by the collar of her coat and head-butted her on her temple. All hell broke loose in the back of the car but Liam came off a lot worse than the girls. He should have remembered what his dad always told him: never get into a fight when you're pissed and your opponent is sober. By the time the girls stopped beating him, his face looked as though it had gone through a mincer.

Liam sat there between two don't-mess-with-me oriental bitches and was he in pain. Thi Kim had thrust her nails into his eyes until he couldn't see a thing, while Thi Le had grabbed his balls and twisted them so hard he felt like she had ripped them off. He had no idea where they were taking him, or why. He could feel moisture trickling down his cheeks but it wasn't tears, it was blood – and it had started to dry on his skin.

The car came to a halt. Doors were opened and he was taken by the scruff of his neck and dragged from the car. As he stumbled and fell, strong hands took hold of him and he was frog-marched into a building. He could hear the bitches' high heels in front of him, leading the way. The next thing he knew he was falling. Over and over he went. He didn't hit every step on the way down but then again, what were a few more bruises to him? He was already a bloody mess. He was lifted and thrown onto a table and his hands were tied.

"Please, no more," he said. "I don't know what you want but whatever it is…" His screams filled the air as a cigarette was put out on his nipple. "For fuck's sake just tell me what you want!"

"Curly boy," Thi Kim said as she walked around the table, letting her fingernails dig into Liam's body as she went. "We want what you know."

"What?" Liam's head lifted off the table as he looked towards the sound of her voice. "Listen, love. Talk fuckin' English and perhaps I can help ya." Thi Le stubbed another cigarette out on Liam's other nipple. "Aaaaahh! What you fucking doing? I told ya I'd help ya. Just tell me what you want!"

"Where you got Ming's skunk? We want it back."

"That's what this is all about, is it? For a start, I haven't got it." Thi Kim picked up a chair and smashed it across Liam's legs. He screamed out, "I've told you I will help you! Just let me finish a bloody sentence!"

"Where you hide it? Tell me or I really hurt you."

"Look, I can tell you where it was, but for all I know Stevie could have moved it by now."

"Stevie who?"

"Stevie Carter."

"Where you take skunk and guns?"

Liam looked panicked. "Guns? What guns?"

"You lie!" Thi Kim yelled at him. She hit him across his shins with a chair leg she still held in her hand.

Liam cried out yet again. "Please, I never saw no guns."

"You lie." Liam felt the full force of her scream just inches from his face.

"I'm not lying to you! I only saw the boxes of skunk in the middle of the warehouse. No … no, wait. That's it! There were two crates. Yeah, two crates – and they were fuckin' heavy an' all."

"Well done, curly boy," Thi Kim said as she smiled to Thi Le. "Where you take them?"

"Don't know the address." Liam tried to look around him for the voice. "I would take you there but there's a problem. You've bloody blinded me, you soppy cow!"

Liam's insult hit Thi Kim like a brick. In her frustration, she started to beat down on Liam again. Thi Le moved in and stopped her by grabbing her arm and speaking to her in her mother tongue. "Stop it! We need him alive." She barked an order to one of the thugs, who was standing there with his arms folded. "You – go get water and bath eye. He's not going anywhere," said Thi Le. "We come back later and talk again."

***

By the time Liam's eyes were healed enough to show them where he and Stevie had stored the skunk and guns, Stevie was long gone on a plane to Cyprus. They beat Liam some more because the warehouse was empty; the skunk and guns were gone. Then they made him take them to Stevie's flat but of course he wasn't there.

Liam was found dead three days later in an industrial waste bin, bloated and wrapped in plastic.

Chapter 18

Alex sat on one of a row of chairs leaning against the wall while his car was being washed. Tony had nipped across the road to get some water as it was a very hot day. As he sat there, Alex could hear the guys cleaning his car talking in a foreign language; he guessed Eastern European, maybe Serb or Croatian, but he didn't have the faintest idea or even care, as they were everywhere.

Tony came out of the shop and darted between two lanes of traffic to get back to the car wash. "Alex!" he called, as he launched the bottle of water towards him.

Alex caught it easily, opened it up and took a long swig to quench his thirst. "Nearly finished," he said to Tony, who was now standing in front of him with his head back, hand in pocket, guzzling from his own bottle in large gulps.

"That's better," he said, wiping his mouth with the back of his hand and grinning back at Alex.

Alex's phone started to ring and he looked down at the screen. "Maxi," he said out loud to no one in particular as he answered it. "Hello Max, what can I do for you?" There was a long pause as Alex listened, and then he said, "See you in half an hour then."

"What's all that about then, Al?"

"Maxi – he wants to see us as soon as."

"Any ideas?"

"No, but it must be important if he wants to see us that quick though." With that, Alex heard one of the guys who was washing his car call to him.

"Boss, all done for you."

"Cheers, Marko." Alex got up and handed him a ten-pound note.

"Thanks boss," said Marko.

Alex and Tony got into the car, started her up and turned

left into Mile End Road. Traffic was light for that time of day. The plan was to meet up with Maxi in the Nelson pub, just off the Hackney Road. When they arrived they found it wasn't the easiest place to find a parking space and they had to park around the corner from the pub.

Maxi was waiting for them at a corner table, a gin and tonic in hand. He stood when they entered. "Al, Tone, what you having?" he said as he shook their hands.

"I'll have a light ale please, Max."

"And you, Tone?"

"Just something to quench my thirst. Tell you what, I'll have a shandy."

"Samantha!" Maxi called to the barmaid. "Light ale and a shandy."

"Half or pint, Max?" she called back.

Maxi looked at Tony. "Half will do," he said.

"Half will do, Sam," Maxi called back. "Oh, bitter or lager, Tone?"

"Doesn't matter."

"Bitter will be fine, Sam. Could you bring them over please? And I'll have another G and T."

The barmaid smiled and said, "Okay."

Maxi chose this pub for the simple reason that it was one of his. In fact, it was one of several he owned. He also knew it wouldn't be packed at this time of day as the dinner time rush was over and there were just half a dozen regulars dotted about the place, staring into their drinks or playing with their phones.

"So what can we do for you, Max?" said Alex.

Maxi sipped his drink before answering. "Best wait until Sam brings over our drinks, and then we can talk without being disturbed."

Alex knew he was right. "How's Mark coming along?"

"He'll be alright, Al, but the Doc said it will be a good

couple of months before he will be able to walk properly again. The bastards really worked him over good."

"Yeah. I heard he was in a real bad way," said Tony.

"He was, but he can see now, thank fuck. You know, I didn't even recognise my own brother when I first saw him sitting there in his office chair, with his hands taped to the arms and nails sticking out of his feet ... and his eyes. God, I don't even like thinking about it. Hold up, here come the drinks." Maxi quickly recovered himself as he saw Sam walking towards them. "Thank you, sweetheart," he said as she placed the drinks down on the table. He gave her a ten and a five and told her to keep the change.

"Ah, thank you, Max." She smiled, turned and made her way back to the bar, leaving them to their business.

"If only I was younger," Maxi said as she walked away. Alex and Tony both followed Maxi's eyes and watched Sam as she walked back to the bar; all three of them were smiling. "Right. Let's get back to why I called you here." Maxi had their attention. "We seem to have a problem."

"In what way?" Alex asked.

"Well, Al, those people who hurt my Mark weren't doing it just for fun. They done it because they were after information. They need to know things."

"Sorry, Max. You've lost me."

"They tortured my Mark to find out about my business – who I work with and what I own!"

"And?" Tony said.

"And, young Tony, they asked an awful lot about my associates."

"Like who?"

"Like you. In fact, they asked lots about you and Alex." Maxi's eyes focused on Alex. "Especially Alex."

"Me? You're joking. Who the fuck are they?"

"That we don't know, but we will find them. So if I were

you I would be keeping my eyes and ears open for anything out of place, anything unusual, because these bastards are out to get each and every one of us. Start asking questions, speak to everyone you know. We have to find them." Maxi picked up the drink that Sam left him and poured it into his glass, then sat back. "Cheers, boys. I think we are at war."

Chapter 19

Tommy had tried all morning to get hold of Colin with no luck, so he rang a few people, but no one had heard from him in days. Tommy was getting frustrated so he gave Colin's mobile one last ring. Nothing. He made up his mind to drop by Colin's place in Butlers Wharf. He didn't think Colin had gone on holiday because if he did, he would have told him. But just in case, he knew where Colin stashed a spare key so he could leave his whack for the month in the flat.

Tommy made his way down the Old Kent Road and turned off towards Tower Bridge. Making a mental note to stop off for some pie and mash in Manze's on the way home, he parked his car around the corner from Colin's apartment and slipped inside a side door that led to the underground car park. As he didn't want the guy on reception to know of his coming and goings, he avoided the security cameras, kept his head down, made his way to the stairwell and started to climb to the top floor.

It may only have been five floors but that was enough to make him short of breath and his legs tired. Tommy felt like an old man: fit for fuck all. He opened the fire door and walked along a short corridor to Colin's apartment, which was on his right. He rang the doorbell. Nothing. Taking a credit card out of his wallet, Tommy placed it in the gap between the architrave and the wall at the top of the door and slid it along until a key fell to the floor. Putting the key in the lock and letting himself in, he waited until the door was closed before he called out.

"Colin? Col, you there?" No answer. Tentatively, Tommy walked along the passageway. He couldn't put his finger on it but something just didn't feel right. "Colin? Natasha?" he called. It wasn't until he reached the kitchen that he realised he could hear a buzzing sound. The kitchen was empty but as he approached the front room, the noise got louder. The room was the size of a football pitch – far too big for his liking, and too modern and minimalistic. The windows ran the whole length of the room and overlooked a large terrace and barbecue area with a view of the river. Tommy called out again. He was starting to think the noise was a record that had got stuck on the turntable; he knew Colin liked to make love to the sound of Wagner's Flight of the Valkyries.

Tommy walked further along the hallway to the bedroom. The door was closed. He put his hand on the doorknob and pushed it open an inch or two. That's when the smell hit him. It was over-powering and he gagged and retched at the same time. Putting his hand to his mouth, he threw the door open. Colin and Natasha were a kinky pair and the bedroom had wall to wall mirrors. He saw their reflection before he saw the bodies. The sound of flies was deafening.

Tommy was fighting hard to keep the contents of his stomach where they should be but he was finding it difficult. He forced himself to enter the room. Blood trails splattered up the walls and across the ceiling, and Colin and Natasha were sitting up in bed, naked. Only something wasn't right... Then he realised what was wrong. They were holding hands, handcuffed together, with their other hands manacled to the headboard. And they were wearing each other's heads. Their eyes told Tommy they had died screaming.

It was a grotesque scene. Their bodies were bloated, with maggots crawling out of their wounds, and the cream satin sheets were drenched in blood. Colin's head was caved in and his eye had been knocked out of its socket and was clinging to his cheek. They both had their legs wide open, and Colin's three piece suite had been cut off and placed in Natasha's mouth, the penis sticking out like a tongue.

Tommy couldn't take any more. He made a dash for the en suite bathroom, tripping over a blood-stained baseball bat on the way. It must have been the one they used to beat Colin.

He just about made it to the toilet. Putting his hands on either side of the bowl, he brought up everything he'd eaten that morning. Out it flowed; he didn't know where it all came from but it just kept coming. When he finally stood up he caught his reflection in the mirror: he looked like death warmed up.

Tommy knew there must be bits and pieces in the flat that would interest the Old Bill but he couldn't bring himself to search the place. He just had to get out of there. Waving away a couple of flies that had followed him into the bathroom, he took some deep breaths. "Come on, Tommy," he said to himself. "Pull yourself together." He washed his face rather noisily, then rinsed his mouth out with some mouthwash he found on the side and dried his face with toilet roll; he didn't want to leave any DNA behind for the police to find. Opening the bathroom cupboard, he found a pair of rubber gloves with some hair dye on them. Must be Colin trying to hide his greying hair by touching it up, he thought.

Picking up a face flannel, he covered it in liquid soap and bleach and proceeded to clean away any evidence of him being in the bathroom. First he flushed the toilet to get rid of his vomit, then he cleaned the pan from top to bottom. He rinsed the flannel out and did the same with the hand basin. He placed the cloth back where he found it, washed the gloves and wiped them clean before putting them in his pocket to dispose of later. He wasn't looking forward to going back past his old friend but he had to get out of there quickly just in case someone called and found him there. He turned to the bathroom door and reached for the handle.

"Shit," he said, realising he still had to touch the doors to get out. Taking the gloves from his pocket, he put them on again. One more deep breath and he swung the door open and rushed across the bedroom, trying not to look at his friend – but he forgot about the mirrors. Covering his eyes to try and shut out the nightmare he found himself in, he reached the door, threw it open and closed it just as quickly. The last thing he wanted was flies following him into the hallway.

Once outside the flat, Tommy took a couple of moments to compose himself. Just as he'd decided to head back for the stairs, he remembered Colin had surveillance cameras hidden in every room. He may have taped his own death – and in doing so also captured his killers. "Fuck!" said Tommy. He froze for a moment, not liking the fact that he had no choice but to go back in. He made up his mind to get in and out of there as fast as he could. He knew exactly where the machine was; Colin had once taken great pleasure in showing Tommy a recording of him and Natasha making love to two of their girlfriends from a sado-masochist club they belonged to. Tommy found it disgusting, not to his liking at all, and he knew if he ever suggested to his Kay that they try any of the things he'd seen that day she would have told him to sling his hook.

He put the key in the door and opened it slightly. Holding it ajar, he placed the key back in its hiding place, counted, "One, two, three," pushed the door open and made his way to the kitchen. Flies swarmed their way into the corridor but Tommy couldn't worry about that. He just had to get the disc. Crouching down by the cupboard next to the fridge, he moved the Cornflakes and Scots Porridge Oats to one side and removed the disc from the machine. There were flies everywhere: on the windows, on the work surfaces; some even landed on his face. Waving the flies away with his arms, Tommy got out of there as quickly as he could, closed the door behind him and made for the stairs without looking back. He put the disc in his pocket and took the gloves off as he walked back down to the car park.

Following the same routine as before, he kept his face turned away from the cameras as he slid out of the side door into the street. Only then did he feel like he was breathing fresh, clean air and he inhaled deeply, hoping no one would notice how pale and shocked he looked. He walked around the corner to where his car was parked and pressed the fob on his key but for a moment he just stood there. Then he noticed a public phone box on the other side of the road. After checking there were no cameras, he made up his mind. He couldn't leave his friend like that. Tommy locked his car back up, crossed the road to the phone box and dialled 999.

He told the police where to find Colin and Natasha but when they tried to ask questions, he just put the phone down. Sweat ran down his brow; his eyes prickled with tears. Tommy took the disc from his coat pocket and turned it over and over in his hands. "I'm going to find you bastards," he said to himself. "There's nowhere you can hide. And when I do find you, you are going to beg me for mercy – but all I will give you is death."

Tommy placed the disc back in his pocket, then wiped the phone and the door handle for prints; he also cleaned the mouthpiece in case he'd left some saliva on the phone. No point leaving any DNA for the police to find. Pushing the door open with his shoulder, he crossed the road to his car. His appetite for pie and mash had gone, so he drove straight home to his Kay.

Chapter 20

Sharon had no idea they were being watched. Then again, neither did Alex. He had promised to treat her for her birthday and they had arranged to meet in Sainsbury's car park at the back of the Blind Beggar pub in Cambridge Heath Road. As she pulled into the car park she saw Alex straight away – but she didn't notice the white Mercedes van two rows back from where Alex was standing next to his car. As Sharon pulled up to greet her son, the people in the white van began to take notice.

"Who is the lady, Mikel?"

"I don't know, Nadia. I have never seen her before. She's very beautiful, I think. No?"

Nadia put her phone down; she would finish her text later. "Yes," she answered. She was bored. They had been following Alex all morning.

"See if you can get close enough to hear what they are saying," Gravel Voice said.

Nadia climbed over Mikel, got out of the van and made her way over to the trolley bay, which was right next to Alex's car. As she approached, she took out her phone and pretended to be having a conversion with a boyfriend.

By now, Sharon had got out of her car and was giving Alex a big hug. Nadia heard Alex greet her as "Mum" and saw him hand over a large wad of notes, which Sharon thanked him for with a kiss. Nadia eavesdropped for a few minutes, then wandered back towards the van, glancing behind once to make sure they were not looking her way. Climbing back into the white Mercedes, she crawled over Mikel into the middle seat.

"Well? What did you learn?" he said, his voice deep and gravelled.

"She's his mother."

"Hey!" He began to chuckle.

"It's her birthday, and he gave her a lot of money."

"Ah, good." He slapped his knee. "I think I will make this woman my bitch."

Nadia found this amusing. "She's old."

He smiled as he lit another cigarette. "No, she's beautiful." The words drifted out of his mouth with the smoke. "I will keep her for a while. Then I will kill her and give her back to him in little pieces."

As he spoke, they watched Alex climb back into his car after giving his mum one last kiss and drive away. Sharon manoeuvred her car into the space he left empty.

"This is good." Gravel Voice leant forward in his seat. "Quick, get ready. We will take her into the back of the van. Nadia..." But Nadia was already out of the door and walking towards Sharon. Mikel get in the back and open the side door, he started the engine and followed her, very slowly.

Sharon had decided as she was already here she might as well get some shopping done. She got out of her car and pressed the key fob to lock it. A white Mercedes van parked next to her but she didn't notice the side door opening. All she felt was a shove in her back before an arm reached out of the van, grabbed hold of her and dragged her inside. Sharon tried to stand up but a man blocked her way. He hit her once on the side of the head and she fell back onto the floor. The van door closed and suddenly there was a woman on top of her, while the man who hit her held onto her arm. She tried to move but she couldn't. "What do you think you're doing?" she cried out. That's when she saw the needle in his hand. She bucked and twisted, kicked out, but it was no use. "No, no!" she screamed. But no one was going to hear her. As the needle went into her arm, Sharon began to cry. The sensation was immediate as she felt the heroin travelling through her veins. Still they wouldn't let her go. The rush ... Sharon had never felt anything like it in her life. Her eyes started to flutter and when she finally went limp in their arms, they released their grip.

Chapter 21

DI Rodney Newman had ordered his usual Chinese takeaway as he walked out of the office. Crispy duck and pancakes, prawn balls, special fried rice, chicken chow mein and a curry sauce; it never varied, always the same. Somewhere between the office and his car, at the far end of the car park, he dropped his mobile – but he wouldn't discover that until later that evening. He decided to pick up some cans from the off licence across the road from the Chinese; he didn't give a monkeys whether it was lager, cider or beer so long as they were on special offer. All that mattered was having something to wash down his takeaway while he relaxed and watched his collection of Laurel and Hardy films. He didn't want to think about anything tonight. He just wanted to enjoy himself.

"I might even ring a brass to come over," Newman thought to himself. He still had a couple of Viagra left in the drawer. All he had to do was give Mikel the Serb a ring and he would send one of his best girls over for nothing. Newman smiled to himself. That was his evening sorted.

DI Newman didn't have a clue that the big boys at the top had decided that enough was enough. They were out to get him and they didn't care how they went about it. He had become a liability and they were worried about just how much dirt he had on them and how he was going to use it.

Chapter 22

Tony leant on the door frame as he watched Joanne in the shower. Arms raised above her head, she rinsed the shampoo from her hair. He could see the nakedness of her flesh through the steam as her body brushed against the glass. She turned and faced him, her eyes closed against the stream of water that cascaded down the length of her body. Tony smiled to himself as she poured some soap from the bottle and, eyes still closed, started to wash her breasts. Cupping them in her hands, she pushed them together then let them go as she slid one hand between her thighs, the other rubbing slow circles over her stomach.

Tony felt the excitement growing down below. He was on his way to joining Joanne in the shower when his mobile started to ring. "Fuck it!"

Joanne called out, "That you, Tone?" She stopped washing herself as she listened for a reply.

"Err yeah, it's me, babe." Tony pulled the phone out of his pocket to see who was ringing him – as if he didn't know. "Alex," he said.

Joanne giggled. "You dirty sod! You've been watching me, haven't you?"

"No, I've just walked in!" Feeling embarrassed, Tony looked up from his phone. Joanne was pressing her body against the glass. Her nipples were erect, clearly begging him to kiss them. He stood there, mesmerised, as The Rolling Stones' ringtone played in his ear: "Start me up, start me up, I'll never stop."

Joanne called out, "Well, are you going to join me or what?" She put her mouth to the shower door and began licking it. Tony looked down at his phone then back at Joanne, who was now moaning playfully, telling Tony what she wanted him to do to her. It was all too much for Tony. Pulling his shirt over his head and throwing it to the floor along with his phone, he advanced towards her, unzipping his trousers as he went. Joanne's hand came out of the door, grabbed hold of the top of his pants and pulled him in.

Tony was grateful the noise of the shower helped to drown out Joanne's over-the-top cries and screams as they made love. For all their play acting and laughter, they both managed to climax simultaneously, Joanne falling to the floor as her legs gave way. Exhausted, Tony managed to pull her to her feet and gave her a long lingering kiss. Smiling at him as they pulled away from each other, Joanne helped him to wash himself clean of her, and he returned the favour.

As he dried her back with the towel, she flicked her hair and hit him in the face. "Sorry!" she laughed. Tony smiled back at her, wrapped her in his arms and kissed her neck. It was at that moment he realised he loved her. The realisation made him stop.

Joanne sensed something was wrong. "Tone, are you alright?" She locked her arms around his waist and looked up into his eyes. "Tony?"

"Sssshh," he said, smiling.

"What is it? You're scaring me!"

"It's you." Tony swallowed and tried to clear his throat.

"What do you mean, it's me?"

"It's you. I love you."

Joanne smiled nervously. "You love me?" she said, looking pleasantly surprised. "You did just say you love me, didn't you?"

"Yes." Tony nodded. He guessed that Joanne, like many girls, had heard those words before. Young fellows would say anything to get their knickers off. But he felt that she knew this was different; as they had made love many times already.

Joanne held her head to one side. "Tony, don't say those words unless you really mean them."

He could see she was being sincere. "Oh I mean it alright, Jo. I've never ever told anyone that I loved them – and I admit it didn't half feel strange when I said it – but I really do love you."

Tears welled up in her eyes. "Let's get this straight." She cleared her throat. "You love me?"

"Correct."

"You don't want to get married or anything like that, do you?"

Tony thought for a moment. "That could be a possibility in the future." He saw her eyes widen, but whether with shock or disbelief, he wasn't quite sure. She leaned back and pressed her hips into him. "Look, I'm not going to ask you to marry me just yet, but I do really love you. There – I said it again. I love you, I love you, I love you, Joanne Parker – with all my heart." She started to cry. "Are those tears of joy?" he asked, concerned. "Only I hope they are."

"Oh Tony, I love you too!"

"Really?"

"Yes, really!"

Tony started to cry and laugh at the same time. Pulling Joanne to him, they kissed a long lingering kiss. Then it happened. "Start me up, start me up, I never stop."

The ring tone broke the magical moment. "That bloody phone of yours. If you really loved me you'd throw it out the sodding window!"

"Then how would Alex get hold of me?"

"See, I knew it wouldn't last," Joanne said.

"Aahh, but he's your auntie's boyfriend and who knows, we could end up having a double wedding."

Joanne looked puzzled. "Tony, I love my Auntie Poppy to pieces. But a double wedding? I don't think so."

"Why not?" Tony was starting to enjoy tormenting her.

"For a start, I don't think my poor dad could take the

strain!"

Tony laughed. "Hello," he said into the phone, as he kissed her bare shoulder.

"Tone! Can't find me mum anywhere!"

"What cha mean, you can't find your mum?"

"Like I said, I can't find her anywhere. It's like she's disappeared. Vanished off the face of the earth."

"What's the matter?" Joanne asked.

Tony put his hand over the phone. "It's Alex. He can't find Sharon. She's missing." He removed his hand. "Al, have you tried your Auntie Ruth's? Perhaps she round there."

"Tried that. She ain't there."

"How long's she been missing?"

"Ain't seen her for three days. I've rung her phone don't know how many times. All it says is unavailable."

"Where did you last see her?" Tony asked.

"Told you – three days ago."

"No, not when, where?"

"Sainsbury's in Cambridge Heath Road. It's not like her not to let me know where she's going, Tone. I tell ya, I'm fuckin' worried, mate."

Tony could sense the anxiety in his friend's voice. "Listen, have you checked the car park?"

"What for?"

"To see if your mum's car is still there, dickhead!"

"No, I haven't," Alex said.

"Well go there now and I'll meet you there. I'll get Joanne to drop me off, alright?"

"Yeah. Okay."

"And Al – don't worry, mate. We'll find her. See you in fifteen." Not giving Alex time to answer, Tony ended the call. His mind was going into overdrive as he tried to figure out what was going on, what with the murders of Colin and his wife Natasha, and Maxi's brother Mark being attacked. He just hoped Alex wasn't thinking the same.

Chapter 23

Sharon felt like shit. She tried to open her eyes but they didn't seem to want to. Her mouth had a terrible taste to it; must have been a heavy night, she thought. Forcing herself to open her eyes and sit on the edge of the bed, she realised then that she hadn't a clue where she was.

"Where the fuck am I?" she said, to no one in particular. Pushing her hair out of her eyes, she looked around the room. It was a dump. There was a bed – if you could call it a bed – with a mattress and a sheet covered in her own vomit, and two pillows that had seen better days. The floor was cheaply carpeted and had even more stains than the bed. Sharon didn't understand why she felt so bad. Then she saw the bruises and needle marks on her arms.

"What the fuck's going on?" The haziness in her head began to clear. "The bastards!" It all came rushing back. The van. The push in the back. A man grabbing her, pulling her into the side door of the Mercedes, punching her. Being held down by a young woman. Seeing the needle go into her arm. Feeling the heroin being injected into her veins. Fucking heroin – that must be 'the rush'. She'd seen Trainspotting. "My God. What fucking nightmare is this? It can't be true. Bloody hell, why me?"

Sharon held her forehead as she stood, swaying. Reaching out with her other arm, she walked towards the window. The view was just a backyard. She tried to open the window but it was screwed down tight and wouldn't budge. The sun was bright and it made her feel lightheaded so she held onto the window sill. "Come on girl, think. Why me?"

Alex was the only thing she could think of. It must be because of him. But why kidnap me, to get at Alex? she thought. That's it – to get at him. To hurt him. So he makes mistakes, gets careless. She leant on the window and rested her forehead on the glass. "Think. Clear your head. Right, for a start I must warn him – but to do that I have to get out of here." Sharon looked around the room for a weapon. "Dressing table – no. Mirror? No – too dangerous. I might badly cut myself. Chair? Yes, the chair!" Moving over to the chair, she picked it up with effort. It was old and not very stable. The stretchers that held the legs together were loose and one of them had a crack in it. If she could break it without making too much noise it would make a good weapon. Placing the chair back on the floor she put her foot on the wood where it was weakest. Pushing down hard, she managed to snap the support but it made a loud crack. She stopped, looked towards the door and listened. Nothing. She did the same to the other chair leg and although she made more noise this time, still no one came up the stairs.

Sharon pulled away a piece of the wood, which left her with a T-shaped handle and an eight-inch long wooden 'stake'. She now had her weapon; it was not much of one but nevertheless, she had a tool that could do the job she needed to do.

Standing at the side of the bed, feet apart like a boxer, Sharon put her right hand behind her back to hide the wooden stake and practised throwing a right cross with the stake sticking out of the front of her fist. She put a lot of effort into the punch but after trying it out half a dozen times it didn't feel right. She switched to using an uppercut punch, which was short, sharp and powerful. Sharon tried hard not to make a noise but each time she threw a punch she blew some air out of her mouth. "Dooff!" On the fourth time of throwing her fist straight up in front of her, she knew that was the one. Feeling comfortable with the weapon she held in her hand, she knew she could do some damage with it. She sat down on the side of the bed to catch her breath and compose herself. Her head was still all over the place but she knew she would only have one go at this – and it had to work first time.

***

Gravel Voice came out of the toilet zipping up his flies, his habitual cigarette hanging from his mouth. Nadia was sitting in the kitchen, resting her arms on the table as she texted, a cold cup of coffee in front of her. Gravel Voice was still trying to do up his flies when one of his phones started to ring. He pulled at the zipper one more time but it wouldn't budge and he caught his shirt in the zip. Frustrated, he reached into his trouser pocket for his phone. "'Da?" he said into the mouth piece. He tapped Nadia's shoulder, pulled a face and pointed to his fly.

She frowned as she glanced up at him, still texting. He clipped her around the back of the head and pointed at his crotch again. Nadia reluctantly put her phone down on the table and set about trying to untangle his shirt from his zip.

Taking the phone away from his mouth and shutting it down, he called out, "Mikel, Zoran." Mikel appeared in the doorway. "Get the car and bring round to front."

"Yes, boss." Mikel moved fast. He could tell his boss was in a hurry.

"Zoran, come here." Zoran did as he was told; he could not read his older brother's thoughts like Mikel and besides – he was afraid of him. "Zoran," said Gravel Voice, taking his little brother's face in his hands. "You have done well since you come over from the old country." Zoran smiled. "So I have a gift for you." Zoran's smile grew even bigger. "I want you to go upstairs and fuck that bitch into submission. Do what you have to do, but break her. You understand?"

Zoran couldn't believe his luck. He had seen them bring Sharon in and even though she was drugged up to the eyeballs and in a terrible state, he knew he had to have her.

Nadia had freed Gravel Voice's shirt from the zip and she pushed him away from her. She had felt his erection getting bigger against her hands as he grew excited at the thought of what his little brother was going to do to Sharon. She went back

99

to her texting.

Gravel Voice let go of his brother's face and, pulling his zip up, told him to check that Mikel was outside with the car. Zoran walked away with a face that said the cat had just got the cream. "Nadia, I want you to make sure he doesn't mark her face," Gravel Voice said. She nodded. "Also, check her phone. There may be something on there that we can use."

"Ok," she said, nodding again.

Gravel Voice heard Zoran call to him, "The car's here."

He put his cigarette out in the ashtray on the ring-stained kitchen table. "And clean this place up. It looks like a pigsty," he said, with a wave of his hand, as he left the room.

Nadia heard the front door close. She was uneasy. She had never liked being left alone with Zoran. His head appeared around the door, a sinister smile spreading across it. "Nadia. Could you make me a needle, please?" he asked.

She stared back at him hard. He may have been her cousin but she didn't like him one bit. "You go easy, you hear me, Zoran?" He pointed a finger at himself as he came into the kitchen, feinting a look of hurt. "I mean it. We don't need another dead one on our hands," she said.

"It was an accident!" he exclaimed.

"So you say, but uncle will not forgive you a second time."

"I can handle my brother." Zoran's tone changed. "Don't tell me what to do. Just make up that fucking needle."

"We'll see." Nadia got up and took a needle from one of the wall cupboards. She unwrapped it from its packaging. Then, taking a bottle of heroin and placing the needle inside, she withdrew just enough to numb the pain this sadistic bastard was going to inflict upon Sharon. "Here." She handed Zoran the syringe.

"Thank you, cousin," he said, taking the heroin from her and a gun from the waistband of his trousers and waving them above his head, mockingly. "Now the fun begins." Zoran giggled to himself as he walked up the stairs.

Nadia called after him, "Remember, don't mark her face."

Zoran stopped. "Don't tell me what to do, bitch," he growled back over his shoulder.

***

Sharon had heard the street door shut just moments before and now she could hear footsteps coming up the stairs. Then a woman's voice, something about 'Don't mark her face', and a man shouting back 'Don't tell me what to do.'

The steps were getting closer. A floorboard creaked. She tiptoed as quickly and quietly as she could back to the bed and sat on the edge of it. Keeping her weapon hidden and out of sight, she waited. A key turned in the door. Sharon took a deep breath and waited, ready to strike like a cobra.

The door opened. Zoran stood there in the open doorway, his silhouette lit up by the light coming from downstairs. "Are you awake?" he said, softly. Sharon could see a gun in his left hand and a syringe in the other. She kept quiet. "If you behave yourself and do as I say, I will not hurt you."

It was then that Sharon realised she knew the voice. "The bastards!" she thought. "I've been here more than a day." Only she couldn't remember how many days she'd been there; she was too far out of it. Still sitting on the bed, she rubbed her eyes as she pretended she had only just woken up.

Zoran left the door open. He wanted Nadia to hear him have his fun. He advanced towards Sharon. "Now give me your arm."

Still pretending to be drugged, Sharon lifted her left arm towards him. Zoran tucked his gun back into his waistband of his trousers so he had both hands free to do the job properly. Big mistake. As he reached out for her arm, Sharon wasted no time. Using all the strength she could muster, she thrust the stake straight into Zoran's throat, under his jaw. She leapt off the bed and pushed him across the room, forcing the stake up into his brain. Blood spurted over her hands and face.

Zoran staggered backwards until he hit the wall by the door. The shock in his eyes said it all. "Fuck! I'm a dead man!"

Sharon saw the needle fall from his hand but he was still holding the gun. Gripping his gun hand, she pulled on his finger and shot him twice in the groin. Then she took hold of his shirt and headbutted him, breaking his nose. As she whipped the gun from his grasp, she shoved him down the stairs, still with the stake embedded in his throat. Sharon pushed him so hard he only connected with the stairs twice on the way down, but he left splatters of blood all the way down the staircase. As he hit the bottom, Sharon was right behind him.

Nadia rushed out to see what had happened, only to find Zoran dead at the bottom of the stairs, his neck broken and a bloodied stake sticking out of his jaw. She looked up at Sharon, who was pointing a gun at her face. "Move!" Sharon commanded. Nadia walked backwards into the kitchen, feeling for the doorframe with her outstretched hands as she went. "You must be the bitch who was in the van. The one who pushed me inside," Sharon said. Nadia said nothing. Sharon saw her phone on the table. "Where's my bag?" Nadia pointed to a cupboard. "Get it." Nadia got the bag and placed it on the table. "Move over there," Sharon commanded again. Nadia went to move around the table to the back door. "No, not there. There by the sink, where I can keep an eye on you." She gestured with the gun. As Nadia moved, Sharon searched her bag, surprised to find the money was still there, as well as her jewellery. She hadn't even noticed she wasn't wearing any.

"Please," Nadia pleaded, "I'm a good girl. I did not want to do this. They made me. They promised my mother I would have good job. But they made me do bad things." She clasped her hands in front of her in the hope that Sharon would believe her and let her go.

Sharon raised the gun. "Tell it to someone who gives a

shit." She shot once, twice. Nadia dropped to the floor, clutching at the wounds in her chest. As Sharon stood over her, panic was written all over her face. She tried to reach out with one hand, the other still trying to stem the bleeding from her chest. "Fucking foreigners," Sharon said, as she shot Nadia between the eyes. Staring down at the woman, she watched as a puddle of blood, growing bigger by the second, started to form around her head.

She moved over to the kitchen sink and, putting the gun down within easy reach just in case, she turned on the tap and proceeded to wash Zoran's blood off her face and hands. Then, opening her bag, she took out her makeup and a lipstick and tried to make herself look presentable, using the kettle as a mirror. She brushed her hair and straightened her clothes. "There," she said. "That will have to do." Picking up the gun, Sharon walked to the front door and opened it to a blast of sunshine. She shaded her eyes and began to walk as quickly as she could. She just wanted to get the hell out of there. She wasn't worried about the police finding the bodies; she knew the arseholes who had kidnapped her weren't going to report anything to the authorities. They would just dispose of the evidence themselves – but she knew there could be comebacks. She had to warn Alex as soon as she could.

Chapter 24

Sergeant King gripped the arms of his chair as he stared at the bottom drawer of his desk. Looking around, he pushed himself a couple of feet away so he was against the wall of the office. He looked around again; no one was taking any notice of him. Taking the keys from his trouser pocket, he reached down and unlocked the drawer. He glanced to the left, then to the right.

"Pull yourself together. What's up with you, Kingy? There's nothing to worry about, you soppy sod." He opened the bottom drawer and took out a phone. Placing it in front of him on his desk, he stared at it as he wondered what he might discover, what terrible secrets it may hold.

DI Newman had been ranting and raging for days now, telling all and sundry what he was going to do to the bastard that had his phone when he found him. King had watched Newman walk to his car in the car park a few days before, had seen the phone fall to the floor, and he hadn't believed his luck when Newman just drove away and left it there on the ground.

It wasn't his work phone; it was one of those new Samsung devices, nearly half the size of an iPad, that you could do all sorts of things with. King picked it up and turned it over in his hands, as if it was some kind of artefact. He didn't know what to do with it. His superiors would be ecstatic when he told them about it, and who knew what the lab boys would be able to get off it. Contacts. Grasses. Perhaps the location of a lock up somewhere where Newman kept his files with all the dirt he had on everyone. Because that was what they had asked him to try and find out about not six months ago, but up till now he had drawn a blank. Perhaps now they could turn the tables on Newman. The DI was a dinosaur, a relic of the past – but he was a dangerous one, and that's what they were afraid of.

Chapter 25

Sharon made her way to the end of the street and found herself in a main road. She looked up at the street sign: High Road N17. She was in Tottenham. She started looking for a ride but quickly realised she would be lucky to find a black cab in Tottenham. Walking further down the road she saw a mini cab office so she went inside to order a car.

The smell of weed lingered in the air. The Rastafarian controller was standing with his back to her, making a cup of coffee. He seemed unaware that Sharon was behind him. She coughed to get his attention. He held a finger up. "Just a moment, lady. I got to get my coffee just right."

Sharon could hear a spoon going round and round in the mug. "Could I have a cab, please?"

"Sure. I nearly there." His voice was very relaxed. "Where you go?"

"Sainsbury's, at the back of the Blind Beggar's in Whitechapel."

He turned and smiled at her. Then, sitting down, he spoke into his mike. "Georgie, come to the office. Lady want to go to Whitechapel."

"Two minutes," came the reply.

"Okay," he said, sipping his coffee.

"Thank you," Sharon said. Still feeling rough, she sat down and looked around the office. The walls were plastered with posters for reggae bands that she had never heard of and adverts for holidays in the Caribbean.

Suddenly, the mike burst into life. "Outside, Robbie."

"Lady. Blue Vauxhall," called the controller.

Sharon walked out to the cab and climbed into the back. The driver was a young black guy who seemed full of himself. "Where we off to in Whitechapel then?" he asked.

"Back of the Blind Beggar – Sainsbury's car park, please."

The cabbie pulled away a bit too fast for Sharon's liking, but she didn't say anything. Taking her phone from her bag, she turned it on and waited for it to fire up. There were missed calls aplenty, nearly all from Alex, with a couple from her friend Jimmy and a few from her sister Ruth.

The cab driver tried to strike up a conversation but Sharon put a stop to it right away. "Your name's Georgie, isn't it?"

"Yeah, that's right." A big smile spread across his face.

"Well, Georgie, I've not been well for the last few days, and I've been out of contact with my friends and family. So what I would like to do is catch up on a couple of things. I'm not being rude, but would you mind keeping your eyes on the road and just drive?"

The driver looked in the rear-view mirror. He didn't like being spoken to like that. "Stuck up bitch," he muttered under his breath.

"And could you turn the music down a bit please?" Sharon asked. This time he gave her a dirty look, as if to say, 'Fuck you, lady.'

Sharon dialled Alex's number from the menu and waited for him to answer. He picked up on the second ring. "Mum! Where the fuck you been? I've been worried sick."

"It's all right, darling," she replied. "I'm on the way to pick up my car."

"It's not there. I had it picked up yesterday."

"What on earth did you do that for?" Sharon exclaimed.

"Mum, you've been missing for three days!"

"What? Three days?"

"Yeah. Three days," Alex repeated.

"The bastards!"

"What do you mean, the bastards? Mum, what's been going on?"

Sharon turned away from the driver and whispered into

the phone, "I was kidnapped."

"You was what?"

"Ssssh! Don't shout." Georgie seemed to straighten in his seat. He looked at her in the mirror, leaning back as he tried to listen to her conversation. Sharon glared at him sternly. "Keep your eyes on the road if you don't mind."

Georgie made a sucking sound through his teeth. As he turned his gaze back to the road he called out, "Shit!" Swiftly, he turned the steering wheel to avoid an oncoming motorbike.

"See what I mean? Eyes forward, please. I'd like to make it to the end of the week at least," Sharon said. She'd pressed her phone against her chest and could hear Alex calling out to her.

"Mum? Mum!"

"Look, I'm okay, Alex. Calm down!"

"Mum, do you know who done it? And how did you manage to get away?"

"Al, I can't really talk right now. I'll explain it all to you later ."

"Did they hurt you, Mum? Because if they did, I'll kill them."

"No, you don't have to worry about that. I got them before they got me," Sharon said.

"What do you mean?"

"I told you, I'll tell you all about when I've been home and cleaned up – but I can assure you it was them that came off worse, not me. I'm a bit shook up, that's all. And tired. I need some rest."

"Mum, go round to my place," Alex said. "Don't argue with me. You're staying with me for now until we sort all this out and find out what the fuck's going on."

"Alex…"

"Mum, I think I know what's going on so please … you'll be safer at mine."

At that moment Sharon put two and two together. The attack on Maxi and Michael's brother. The deaths of Colin and Natasha. Who were these people? It was then that even she felt afraid – not just for herself, but also for her son. "Alex, meet me at the bagel shop in Brick Lane," she said. "I'm bloody starving. I've had nothing to eat for days."

"How long will you be?" he asked.

She put her hand over the mouthpiece. "Georgie, how long would it take to get to Brick Lane, Bethnal Green end?"

"With this traffic, could be forty minutes," the driver replied.

"Do it in thirty and I'll give you a twenty-five quid tip." Sharon felt the car accelerate. "Alex, I should be there in half an hour and I'll tell you everything that happened, okay?"

Alex agreed to her request. Sharon told him she loved him and on hearing his reply, she ended the conversation. A tear started to trickle down her cheek. She turned away from the driver so he wouldn't see she was crying, and stared into the emptiness of the sky.

Chapter 26

The funeral cars were lined up outside the home that Leon had known all his life. He had given his family nothing but love, and now they in return were showing how much he had meant to them. As the coffin emerged from the front door, the local press were being as discreet as they could, taking their photos from across the road, their backs against the railings of Victoria Park.

Randall and Pete were the lead pallbearers, followed by Randall's brothers Tommy and Jackson. The other two were Leon's friends: Sam, who played drums in Leon's band, and Hughie, his best mate from the Arsenal youth team. He was going to be cremated at the East London Crematorium in Wanstead Flats. As they descended the steps from the family home, a gospel choir from the local Pentecostal church started to sing 'Amazing Grace' from across the street. It brought tears to Pete and Randall's eyes. Leon used to be a member of the church youth club and his band practised in their basement, so it was nice of them to come and see off one of their own in full voice.

Leon's mum followed the coffin down the steps, holding onto her daughter Rachel for support. Behind her were her two sisters-in-law, assorted cousins and other family members. People lined both sides of the street. Some were genuine mourners; others were just there to be seen.

Under the guidance of the funeral director, who wore a top hat and caped coat and held a silver-topped black staff, the pallbearers placed the coffin in the back of the hearse, and the funeral director's team swiftly placed floral arrangements around it. On top of the coffin was a spectacular arrangement of flowers that covered the whole coffin lid, and along the sides, decorations spelled out 'Leon', 'brother' and 'son'. Soon the inside of the hearse was a sea of colour. But pride of place went to a big football in the Arsenal colours, studded with individual cards signed by all the players, which went on top of the hearse. It took some time to secure it to the roof. Arsenal's manager, Arsene Wenger, had sent his apologies for not being there as the team had a game up north, but they were still well represented by some famous old players, Charlie George and Ian Wright among them, along with coaching staff and fans wearing the club colours.

Randall walked along the street, shaking people's hands and thanking them for coming and paying their respects. Pete started to do the same, except he quickly moved further and further away from the main body of the funeral, slipped into the back of a waiting Jaguar and disappeared around the corner. Inside the car, Alex leant across from the front seat and shook Pete's hand. "Sorry about your brother."

"Thanks Al." Considering what he was about to do, Pete was surprised he didn't feel nervous.

"So, you up for this?"

"I'm cool." Alex looked deep into Pete's eyes. "Honest, I'm fine."

Alex turned back and faced the road. "Okay, we know where the arseholes are. Your brother's friend Kieran rang ten minutes ago. Three of them are in a Somalian café down the Roman Road. They're the ones who stabbed your brother." Pete shook his head. Alex continued: "The other two Kieran will take care of. He knows where they live."

Tony, in the driver's seat, turned the car into an old railway arch, one of many in the Hackney area. As they got out of the car Alex walked over to a bench, opened a box and called to Pete, "Here you go." He threw a set of motorbike leathers at him. "Change into these."

Pete held them up; they seemed the right size so he changed into them as quickly as he could. He looked around and saw the guns they were going to use lying on top of a work bench.

"Boots," Tony said. A pair of motorbike boots fell at Pete's side. As he sat down to try them on, a train went over the bridge above them, making him flinch. The fluorescent lights above shook violently.

Once he had changed clothes, Tony walked over to the workbench. "Pete," he said, as he examined the weapons, "you can have one of the machine guns. That way you should get all of them with one spray. But don't worry – Alex will be right behind you and I will be outside, making sure no one interferes."

The atmosphere was weird; they were all so calm. Alex tapped Pete on the shoulder. "Come on. Let's go." Pete zipped up his leathers and walked over to the workbench. "Put these on as well," Alex said, giving him a pair of driving gloves. "Now pay attention." He put a double magazine into the machine gun. "This is held together with duct tape so you don't have to mess about releasing one magazine and finding another. You just spin it round, slam it in and you're ready to go again." Alex showed him how to do it . "You got it?"

"Yeah."

"Okay, you have a go." Pete pressed the button releasing the clip, turned it round, and slid it back in place. "Good. Well done," Alex said. He took the gun off Pete, put it on full auto and applied the safety catch – just in case Pete pulled the trigger by accident. "All you have to do is safety off, point and pull the trigger – and all hell breaks loose. Okay?" Pete nodded. "Look, let me show you the best way to hold it. Remember, two hands – none of that Brixton gangster lark of one hand and everyone within a thousand yards gets a bullet up his arse. Because when you fire this bloody thing it starts to climb, so you have to control it. Short burst, and don't leave your finger on the trigger. Not that you have to worry about the ammo. We've got plenty of it." Alex put his hand on Pete's shoulder. "You alright?"

"Yeah, I think so," Pete said.

"Good. Because me and Tony will be right there backing you up, so there's no chance you're going to fuck this up, alright!" Standing like a boxer, feet slightly apart and leaning on his front foot, Alex moved his body from side to side as if he was firing the gun. "Just do it like this and you will be okay." Pete nodded and copied Alex's moves. "That's it," Alex said, as he put the gun into a shoulder bag. "You're on the back with me. You ever ride pillion before?"

"Yeah, loads of times."

"Good. You know what to do then." Alex handed Pete the bag. "Let's go."

They mounted the bike. Tony opened the gate to the arch and let Alex out first. Then he pushed his bike into the street, put it on its stand and closed the gate. Then, climbing on his bike, he made sure his rucksack was secure and started up the engine. Two powerful Kawasakis disappeared into the mid-morning traffic.

***

At the same time, Leon's friend Kieran, carrying a two gallon can of petrol in a Tesco bag, was getting out of the lift on the top floor of a tower block. There was no one in sight. Looking around him, he walked along the corridor until he found the right door. As he knelt down and looked through the letter box, he saw a figure walk in front of him into the front room. The smell of skunk hit him straight away. "Good," he thought, "a bit of luck. They won't know anything until it's too late." He pulled some plastic tubing and a funnel out of the bag and pushed one end into the letter box until all six feet of it had disappeared. As he started to pour petrol into the funnel, some of it spilled onto his hands and he was glad he was wearing gloves. It seemed like an eternity till the can was empty. Handily for Kieran, some of the petrol started to seep out under the door He heard someone shout out something in Somali. Quickly, he struck a match and let it drop to the floor. It caught light straight away.

The young Somali drug dealer was standing in the middle of the hallway of the flat, his bare feet soaked in petrol. He didn't stand a chance. He tried to shout out a warning to the others but it was too late. He heard a whoosh as the wall of flames came rushing towards him. Turning to run, he had nowhere to go. The flames engulfed him. He staggered into the front room, screaming, and fell at the feet of his friends, who, on seeing their friend in flames, panicked. The flat was an inferno in seconds.

Kieran rode the lift down to the ground floor and casually walked out of the entrance of the block of flats. Lying in front of him was a burning Somalian, who must have fallen to his death trying to flee the flames. Kieran laughed as he looked up and saw smoke billowing from the top floor. "For you, Leon," he said. Then he threw his arms out wide and cried: "Rastafari for you, my brother!" As he walked away he lit up a joint and smiled.

***

Pete saw the café a hundred yards in front of him. Two men were standing outside, arguing and waving their arms about. Tony pulled up next to them, got off his bike and straightened his rucksack so he could pull out his gun if it was needed. Alex parked alongside him. Pete was so pumped up nothing was going to stop him from taking revenge for his brother's death. As he reached into the shoulder bag, the two men spotted the gun. They turned and ran off as fast as they could. Pete looked into the café; there were eight people inside. They all looked spaced out on chat, a kind of leaf that, when chewed, gave the same high as speed. The three he wanted were sitting at a table in the back. He handed the bag to Alex, who took out his gun and followed Pete through the door. Tony stood guard outside. Alex noted that Pete seemed relaxed as he turned the safety catch off.

As they entered the café Pete could see the terrified look on the men's faces, even through the narrow slit of the motorbike helmet's visor. He spotted movement on his right, but the man didn't even have time to get out of his chair before Alex shot him, spraying blood onto the wall behind. At the sound of the gunshot, Pete's brother's killers turned towards him. One of them jumped up and threw his chair to one side as he tried to get away. Pete shot him first. Then all he could see was flames and smoke from the gun as the bullets spat out of the end of the barrel. He had forgotten all about the short bursts Alex had told him to do, but he held the weapon tightly and moved his body from side to side until the first clip was empty.

So far, he'd killed five people. The café owner was slumped on the floor where he had fallen behind the counter, boiling water pouring from the tea urn onto his listless body. Two of his customers sat dead at their table, both with holes in their heads; they were just in the wrong place at the wrong time. Two of Leon's killers never left their seats; they didn't even get to see who shot them.

But the third killer – the one who tried to run away – was still alive. Pete released the magazine and turned it round, making sure it was secure. Then he walked back through the smoked-filled café and stopped in front of his brother's killer. The man's life blood was already spilling out of a wound in his neck. Pete cocked the gun and said: "This is for my little brother." Time seemed to slow down as he pointed the gun and fired it, one-handed. He watched in slow motion as the bolt slid up and down, pumping six bullets of death into the terrified face of his brother's killer, sending him to meet his maker. Then, turning to the other two, he put two more bullets into their backs just to make sure.

Pete surveyed the carnage he had just wreaked in front

of him. Amidst the smoke and dust lay six bodies, and numerous holes in the walls that surrounded him. He heard Alex call to him: "Come on, we're done here. Let's go." As he started walking back towards the café door, he saw two more bodies slumped at a table. He knew Alex had shot someone but hadn't realised how many. As he left the café he could see people transfixed, staring through the windows in shock, not quite sure what they had just witnessed.

Tony and Alex were already on the bikes, motors running. Pete walked past two women with shopping bags at their sides, their mouths wide open. He took no notice of them and got on the back of the bike behind Alex. Putting the gun away in the shoulder bag, he tapped Alex on the back and they roared away, leaving mayhem and death behind them.

**

The service had already begun when Pete walked in, playing with the flies of his trousers to make it look like he had just been to the toilet and not murdering his brother's killers in Bethnal Green. He went straight to the front of the congregation and sat down next to his father. Randall glanced sideways at his remaining son, who just nodded. Without Pete saying anything, Randall knew justice had been served. He squeezed Pete's hand as the reverend preached tolerance in the community and introduced a song by Marvin Gaye. "Listen to Brother Marvin's words and save the children," the reverend said.

The choir sang: "Amen."

The reverend replied, "Because they are our future."

The music began and Marvin started to sing. "I just want to ask the question, who really cares? To save a world in despair."

While his words rang out in the tiny chapel, it was the sound of sirens that rang out back in Bethnal Green, where all hell had broken loose.

Chapter 27

DI Newman had had enough of being given the run around by everyone. He wasn't happy with the answers he was hearing. He hadn't seen Bobby Makin in months yet whenever he asked anyone about him, no one seemed to know a thing. The last time they'd spoken was when Newman phoned Bobby at his fiftieth birthday party to spoil his evening and wind him up, and that was six months ago.

The detective inspector was sitting in his office with his feet up on the desk, rolling sheets of paper into balls and throwing them into a waste paper basket. He was bored. "Where the fuck are you, Makin, you scum bag?" he yelled. "You can't hide from me. I will find you wherever you are!" He shouted so loud the other officers, sitting the other side of the glass panels around his office, turned and stared. "What you fuckin' lot looking at? Go on, get on with your work and don't be worrying about me!" Newman rocked back and forth in his chair as he grumbled to himself, "And if that bastard hasn't got a good enough excuse for his absence I'm going to take him down. I don't care if he is the best grass I've ever had – he's taking the piss! And besides, I'm retiring soon anyway and this way I can go out with a bang." He rolled up another scrap of paper and tossed it into the bin. "Yes!" he shouted. Then, picking up his paper coffee cup, he drained it in one go and rested it on his belly.

Constable Perry tapped on his office door and entered. "Guv..."

"If you ain't got good news for me, son, you can fuck off as well. Because I'm not taking any shit from no one today."

"I don't know about good news, guv, but I've just seen Sharon Dicks – or should I say Sharon Makin – getting out of a lovely new Merc sports car outside her house."

"Really? So what do you want me to do about it?" the DI

scoffed.

"Nothing. I was just saying I just saw her, that's all."

"So that's big news, is it? I'm looking for her bloody husband and you're telling me the flash bitch has got a new car?"

"Sorry, I..."

"Fuck sorry!" Newman got to his feet and grabbed his coat off the back of the chair. "Where's Kingy?"

"Don't know, guv."

"Looks like you'll have to do then. Come on," Newman said as he walked past Constable Perry, brushing a uniformed bobby out of his way. Perry, hurrying after Newman, had to step around a very angry young officer who was glaring at Newman's back. As they got to the car park Newman threw the keys to Perry. "You drive."

"Where to, guv?"

"To the flash bitch's place, where else?" came the reply.

The traffic was light so it didn't take them long to get to Sharon's house. They parked across the road from her front door. Sharon's car was outside. As they stopped, Newman flew out of the car and rushed across the street towards Sharon's door. Perry, fumbling to lock the car, did his best to keep up with the detective inspector.

**

Sharon had sneaked out of Alex's house to pick up some dry cleaning she'd left weeks ago; it was the first chance she'd had since the kidnap. Alex wouldn't let her go anywhere by herself unless she had Jimmy the Veg or Billy Boy Spencer at her side. Knowing there were only a few parking bays near the shops, she'd parked her Merc right outside her house and walked to the dry cleaner's. She knew Alex would go mad when he found out she had given Jimmy the slip; she had told her guard she wasn't going anywhere and if he wanted he could have the afternoon off.

Having collected her dry cleaning, she returned to the car. As she turned the corner she saw Newman banging on her door. At first she thought he was by himself. Then she saw Constable Perry hurrying across the road to join him. What happened next took her – and DI Newman – completely by surprise.

***

"Open up, this is the police!" The street door was flung open and two men in leather bomber jackets appeared. Newman called out, "Who the bloody hell are you two?" He hadn't noticed the guns in their hands and it was too late when he did. As the first man came at him firing his gun, Newman stepped back, only to feel the bullets hitting him, one in his shoulder, the other in his arm. He fell against Sharon's car, just managing to keep his balance as he called out to Constable Perry, "Run, they've got guns!" But Perry was standing there frozen, petrified and open-mouthed. As Newman staggered towards him he felt a third bullet hit him in the other shoulder, but the fourth he didn't feel as it shattered his spine and ricocheted into his heart, killing him before he hit the ground. The second gunman fired the final shot, sending Perry to his knees holding his stomach.

Sharon just stood there, staring in horror. She watched the gunmen run off around the corner and come speeding back in their getaway car, which headed off at high speed, burning rubber all the way and leaving a cloud of smoke in its wake.

Then she heard Perry calling out for help. She knew she should have got out of there fast, but how could she leave that poor boy – who was only a couple of years older than her Alex – to die by himself, alone in the middle of the road? She knew the gunmen weren't coming back. "Sod it," she said. Besides, this had happened outside her house. If she ran away the police would come looking for her. She rushed to the constable's side. Throwing her cleaning over the bonnet of her car, she knelt

118

down and pushed Perry onto his back. Knowing that she had to try and stop the bleeding, she took off the hoody she was wearing and pressed it hard onto the wound. Then she took out her phone and rang for the emergency services. They asked her all sorts of questions, which she answered as quickly as she could, but it seemed her answers were not to their liking. In the end, she told them to get their bloody arses in gear and ended the call. She knew she had to tell her Alex she was in trouble – and she needed a lawyer fast.

Chapter 28

Little Jimmy was getting on with his life. He was never going to be fully fit like before but he was giving it a go. His walking had improved a hundred per cent and he was enjoying being with Sharon. He was feeling alive for the first time in years, and looking after Sharon made him feel so good. He didn't quite know if he could actually do anything if it came to it but he would give it a go; he would do anything for Sharon. At last he was doing something with his life: Billy Boy looked after Sharon Mondays, Tuesdays and Wednesdays and he took care of her the rest of the week.

He knew Sharon had always had a soft spot for him, even though he knew it would never be more than that. It didn't stop him loving her, and if it meant laying down his life for her, he would do it in the blink of an eye.

He had started to play guitar again, and was surprised how quickly it all came back to him. He was sitting there in his front room playing the blues like his hero Pete Green and singing a Robert Johnson song:

"I got a kind-hearted woman, do anything in this world for me.

Got a kind-hearted woman, do anything in this world for me.

But these evil-hearted women, they will not let me be.

I love my baby, my baby don't love me."

His phone started to ring. He leaned over and saw that it was Alex. He stopped playing and picked it up. "Hello?"

"Where are you?"

"I'm at home, Al."

"Well what the fuck you doing there? You're supposed to be with Mum!"

"She told me to go home as she wasn't going anywhere."

Jimmy pulled the phone away from his ear and stared at it,

hard. Alex sounded so worried.

"Well she changed her fuckin' mind and all hell has broken loose!" he said.

"What do you mean?" Jimmy asked, confused now.

"DI Newman just got himself shot outside Mum's house. He's dead."

"What?"

"And Mum saw it all. She's been took down to the Old Bill station!"

"Oh Al," Jimmy said. "I'm so sorry. I…"

"Look, don't worry about it – but fuck, mate, you should have been there. I gave you a job and you…"

"Al, I will make it up to you," Jimmy said.

"Too right you will!" Alex replied. "Right …err… I've got to go. I'll give you a bell. Ring Billy and tell him what's happened."

"Alright Al, I'll ring him right away. I'm so sorry."

Alex realised he was wrong to bollock Jimmy; it wasn't his fault. "Jim."

"Yeah?"

"Sorry, mate."

Chapter 29

When the news came through that a police officer had been shot, Sergeant King sat motionless at his desk. When he heard DI Newman had been shot and killed and a young police officer called Perry was in a critical condition, he was speechless. Alright, he and every other policeman in the station disliked Newman; in fact, to a man they all hated him. But he was still one of their own, and that poor kid ... and he was just a kid; he was only 29 years old, after all.

Sitting there staring out of his window, he started to wonder what the tech boys had found on DI Newman's phone – if it had revealed his sources, or even where he had stored the files he was supposed to have on everyone. Knowing Newman, he would have hidden them away where no one would ever find them.

King's desk phone rang , making him jump. He let it ring a couple more times before answering. "Sergeant King."

It was DI O'Neil. "King."

"Yes."

"Get ready."

"Get ready for what, ma'am?" King asked.

"I need to know everything you know about Sharon Makin."

"And why's that, ma'am?"

"Because the bloody gunman who shot DI Newman came out of her bloody house, that's why!"

Sergeant King couldn't quite believe what he had just heard. What he knew about Sharon Makin didn't make her a killer. She was tough alright, but a killer? He didn't think so. "Are you saying Sharon – I mean, Mrs Makin – killed DI Newman?"

"No, that's not what I mean," O'Neil said, "but what we do know is that DI Newman and Constable Perry went there to talk to Mrs Makin. She wasn't there but the two gunmen were, and they came out of her house guns blazing and shot Newman and Perry just as Mrs Makin came around the corner."

"So Sharon had nothing to do with the shooting?"

"We don't bloody well know! But that's what we are going to find out. They are bringing her here for questioning, and I need to know everything about her. I understand you've know her for a long time?"

"Course I know her. She's been married to two of the biggest armed robbers around!" King said. "But I'm not her friend. I just know her," he added.

"Well, that's more than I know! Look, I'll be along in about ten minutes and you can fill me in with whatever you have. We don't have much time."

"Ok, I will see what I can do," King replied. He put the phone down on DI Jennifer O'Neil. He couldn't make his mind up about her. It didn't bother him that he had to take orders from a woman; she seemed good at her job even if she was pushy. In fact, she was one of the rising young stars being fast tracked through the ranks. Whereas he had been a copper for ten years longer than her – but his face just didn't fit for promotion. He wasn't pretty enough, or maybe he just hadn't rubbed shoulders with the right people, the funny handshakes mob: the force was full of them.

But he did have one thing up his sleeve that they didn't. He had been working with the slipperiest bastard ever to be in the Metropolitan Police Force: DI Newman. And he had learnt an awful lot from him over the years.

Chapter 30

Most people would be worried sick to be in Sharon's predicament, but not Sharon. She realised that this was a great opportunity to lay the blame for Bobby's death at someone else's door. While she was waiting to be interviewed she'd been going over and over her story in her head – and knowing that DI Newman was dead was a big bonus.

She had done her best to help the young policeman, firstly because she took pity on him as he was so young, but also because it wouldn't do her any harm in the police authority's eyes to have been seen to be helping to do her best to stop the officer from bleeding to death. While attending to PC Perry, who was about her Alex's age, she had rung her son to tell him what had just happened and to ask him to get her brief to her as soon as possible.

She heard the door open behind her. Sergeant King came in and stood across the desk from her. Sharon looked up at him and smiled. "Hello, Sharon," he said.

"Sergeant King."

"Well, I don't quite know where to begin. This is a right old mess!"

Sharon still had a smile on her face. "I don't know. I thought you lot would be jumping for joy like the rest of us now that DI Newman is dead."

"And what makes you think that?" King said, a half-smile on his face.

"Oh come on. I bet there's as many coppers out there as villains raising a glass now the bastard's gone!"

King's face broke into a broader smile. "Off the record, yes. But he is still a serving police officer."

"Was," Sharon shot back.

King pulled a chair out from under the table and sat down. A strong smell of perfume hit Sharon from behind;

perhaps she hadn't noticed it before because her thoughts were elsewhere. Then the wearer of the perfume came into view. "Sharon, this is DI Jennifer O'Neil," Sergeant King said.

A tall, striking redhead came around the table and looked down at Sharon. "Hello, Sharon," she said holding her hand out. Taking in the officer standing before her, Sharon could tell this woman took no nonsense. Just as DI O'Neil was about to drop her hand, Sharon leant forward and shook it limply before settling back down into her chair. "Can we offer you some tea or coffee before we begin?" the DI asked.

"You can get me a large glass of water if you like, but I won't be answering any of your questions until my brief gets here."

DI O'Neil looked at her sharply. So that's how it was going to be. She sighed. "Sharon, all we want to know is what happened today. We aren't here to charge you with anything."

Smiling back at the DI, Sharon fired back, "That's why I'm waiting for my brief to advise me. Because you never know where this could lead. Yes, I admit I was a witness to a police officer's murder. But what I don't know was why DI Newman was banging on my door and shouting at the top of his voice. And secondly, what the fuck were those men doing in my house in the first place?"

With that, there was a knock on the interview room door. "Yes?" called out the detective inspector. It was only one word but already Sharon could tell this redhead had a fiery temper.

A young constable peered around the door. "Sorry, ma'am, but Mrs Makin's solicitor is here."

The DI's knuckles turned white as she stared at Sharon across the desk. "That's all we need." King shrugged in response. O'Neil stood, dragged her hand through her hair and said. "Let him in."

***

Alex was waiting outside with Sean Reilly, Sharon's brief, when the young constable came over to them. It was obvious he didn't know who Alex was as he asked them both to follow him. Alex exchanged glances with Sean but said nothing. They followed the constable to the interview room, where he knocked on the door and waited for a reply.

"Come in," called Sergeant King.

Alex was first through the door. Pushing past the constable to get to his mother, she stood to greet him. He cuddled her in his arms. "You alright?"

"Yes, I'm fine," Sharon said.

DI O'Neil was surprised that a brief would embrace a client in such a manner. Then, seeing Sean Reilly walk into the room behind Alex, she exploded. "Who the bloody hell is this, and how did he get in here?"

Sean walk past Alex and Sharon, placed his briefcase on the table and introduced himself. "Hello, my name's Sean Reilly. I represent Mrs Makin." He held his hand out to her.

O'Neil shook it, but she was shaken to see Sean standing there in front of her. She had only left his bed not five hours ago. They had been having a relationship for the last six months and, naively, she had thought their paths would not cross professionally. Now she felt stupid having to shake his hand and make out she didn't know him. "Right," she said, regaining her composure. "I want him out of here now." She pointed to the door.

"Oh come on, Jennifer." Sean smiled at her.

"The name's DI O'Neil." She gave him a stern look. Then she glanced at Sergeant King, who had decided to shuffle some papers around He didn't want to get involved.

"Mrs Makin has been through a terrible experience, DI O'Neil," Sean said. "At least let her see her son so he can comfort her before we convene."

"Please," said Sharon, looking at the DI with doe eyes. "It would help me if I could speak to my son in private – and have a consultation with my brief."

Sergeant King stood up. "I think that would be an excellent idea, ma'am." DI O'Neil looked at him as if to say, 'Are you fucking kidding me?' Unperturbed, King continued. "She has been through an awful lot, and I think it will help her to be more relaxed and cooperative in the long run, so I feel a short break would help, don't you?" O'Neil wasn't happy but she could see that her sergeant's course of action could be to their benefit. Flicking her hair over her shoulder, she turned on her heels and stormed out of the room, followed by King.

Sean waited until the door was closed before asking Sharon, "I know I've no need to ask but you haven't said anything, have you?"

Sharon gave him a 'Come on, what do you take me for?' look before answering with a simple "No."

"Good. I didn't think you would. So what I propose is we sit down and go through exactly what you need to say."

Sharon nodded. She sat down with Alex by her side and they talked for thirty-five minutes before Sean was satisfied she was ready to give her statement to the police.

Chapter 31

DI O'Neil was finding it hard to sit and wait for Sharon to prepare herself for questioning. It shouldn't be happening like this; it wasn't the way it was supposed to be. She was a very impatient woman who liked to get her own way and God help anyone who got in hers – because at this moment in time she felt that she had lost control of the situation, that Sharon was in control instead of her.

The young constable walked into the canteen. "About bloody time," she said, getting up and pushing past him before he had even spoken. King followed her out of the room. He shrugged his shoulders at the young PC and gave him an embarrassed smile.

When they walked into the interview room the atmosphere was very calm and relaxed, but O'Neil was about to change that. "Right, let's get this started, shall we?" She was like a bull in a china shop.

O'Neil and King sat down as Alex got up. "I don't think you will be needing me anymore, but if you do you can get hold of me through my solicitor, Mr Reilly."

"I don't think you will be needed, Alex, so that's fine by us," said Sergeant King.

Alex rested his hand on Sharon's shoulder. "Give us a call, Mum, and I will pick you up. You can stay with me for now. This lot won't be finished at your place for a while."

Sharon nodded as Alex gave her a kiss on the cheek and left. She settled in her seat and Sergeant King turned on the tape recorder. "Time is 16.00 hours on the 25th August. Subject is Mrs Sharon Makin..."

Hoping to upset the proceedings, Sharon interrupted him. "So," she said, "where do you want me to start, Jennifer?"

"DI O'Neil will do. Let's keep this on a professional basis, shall we?"

Sharon smiled back at her, flicked her hair over her shoulders and said, "Ask away."

O'Neil leaned into her first question. "So why do you think these men were in your house?"

"That I don't know, but I think I know why DI Newman was."

"Oh yes, and what was he there for?"

"He was looking for my Bobby."

"And why would he be doing that?"

"Because Bobby has gone missing, and no one can find him," Sharon said.

That got King's attention. "What do you mean, Sharon – no one can find him? Has he gone abroad? Spain, perhaps?"

"No, he's just disappeared. I haven't seen him in months."

"Are you saying you think he has left you?"

"I don't know what I'm saying," Sharon said. "With all the strange things that's been going on lately, who knows what's happened to him!"

"I'm sorry, Sharon," said DI O'Neil, "but how long has your husband been missing?"

"Well, that's the question, you see? I don't know if he is. But the last time I saw him was the morning after the birthday party I threw for him. I left for Portugal that morning with my friend Marsha and Bobby was supposed to follow us out there. But he never arrived – and I haven't seen him since."

"You still haven't answered my question, Sharon." DI O'Neil was getting angry with Sharon's behaviour. "How long has he been missing?"

Sharon tried to look hurt. She took a deep breath before answering the detective inspector. "That was nearly five, all 6 months ago."

"Five months!" DI O'Neil barked, putting her hands on her hips. "My God, and you didn't think it was appropriate to report his disappearance to the police?"

"No, I..." Sharon stopped and paused. As if on cue, her brief leaned in close and whispered in her ear. She nodded and glanced at the two detectives, then went back into a huddle with Sean. "Do you think that's the best thing to do?" she asked him. Sean nodded. Sharon flicked her hair over her shoulders again, then turned to face them. Resting her fingertips on the edge of the table, she said: "I think my Bobby's dead."

Sergeant King responded first. "And why do you think that, Sharon?"

She looked deep into the sergeant's eyes. "Well, he never arrived in Portugal. At first I thought he had run off with another woman."

DI O'Neil interrupted. "Who's the other woman?"

"I don't know," Sharon said, "but I know he had one not too long ago. He denied it, of course."

"When?"

"About six months before he vanished. I told him to finish with her or I would cut his balls off. He still insisted he hadn't been with anyone else but you just know, don't you, Jennifer?" This was Sharon's chance to start laying a false trail about Bobby's disappearance.

"And you never found out who it was?"

"No – and I didn't want to."

"Do you think it was someone you know?" O'Neil asked.

"No, but I think it may have been someone in one of the massage parlours he has a piece in. But then again, quite a few of his friends have been murdered lately, so I was leaning more towards that as a possibility. Everyone's having trouble with these bloody foreigners – they're trying to take everything over!"

The two police officers looked at each other; they knew there was some truth in what Sharon was saying. "So, Sharon," DI O'Neil continued, "you're saying your husband has been killed by rival criminals? Was it over a drug deal gone wrong?"

O'Neil raised her voice and leant forward as she tried to intimidate her witness.

Sharon laughed back at her. "Where the fuck did you get this amateur from, Kingie? Because if this is the way this interview is going to be conducted, I will refuse to talk to this idiot and only talk to you!"

"You bitch!" spat DI O'Neil.

"Fuck you!" Sharon shouted back.

Both Sergeant King and Sean could see things were getting way out of hand. "Now, now, ladies," said King.

"That's no fucking lady!" retorted DI O'Neil as she turned and walked to the back of the room.

"I'm not taking this shit!" Sharon said. "This interview is over."

O'Neil spun around to face Sharon. "This interview ain't over until I say it is."

"As I said before – fuck you!" Sharon stuck two fingers up to the detective inspector. Then she started to collect her things, stood up and walked towards the door.

"Sit down! I haven't finished with you yet."

King couldn't believe what was happening, but he knew he had to regain control. "This is Sergeant King terminating the interview."

Sharon's brief stood up. "As my client isn't under arrest I think it's best if we leave and try and do this another day." He walked towards the door, then stopped. "Oh, by the way. I will be making a complaint to your superiors as your behaviour has been appalling."

Jennifer, open-mouthed, looked shocked at what she had just heard. She called after Sharon's brief. "Sean."

"No. I'm sorry, Jennifer. You took this too far."

Sergeant King looked puzzled as he watched Sean leave the room. He was even more confused when DI O'Neil started to hit the wall with her fist. "Fuck, fuck, fuck!" she yelled.

King got up and started to run after Sharon. "Mrs Makin!" Sharon kept walking. "Sharon, please wait."

Sean put his hand on Sharon's shoulder but she shook it off. "Sharon, let's hear what he has to say." She stopped.

Sergeant King realised he had another chance. "Sharon, please let me talk to you. Just me."

She turned round and pointed at him. "You and no one else. My house, 10 o'clock tomorrow." She took a few steps towards him and poked him in the chest. "And if I see that fuckin' bitch anywhere near my house – no interview. Got it?"

"Got it."

"Because that's where you're going to interview me. So get your fuckin' forensics out of my home and make sure there's no bugs. I will be having it swept before I say a word."

"You have my word, Sharon. Just you and me." Sean tilted his head, as if to say 'What about me?' "And of course Mr Reilly." Sharon gave Sergeant King one last stern look. Then she turned on her heels and walked away. Once she was through the police station door she smiled. Sharon had got what she wanted: total control of the situation.

King walked back into the interview room. "Well, what's happening?" O'Neil said, throwing her hands in the air.

"What's happening is Mrs Makin will have nothing to do with you."

"She'll do as she's fucking well told!" O'Neil screamed.

"You just don't learn, do you?"

"What?"

It was King's turn to lose his temper. "For fuck's sake, Jennifer. Back off!"

"Don't you dare talk to me like that!"

"You blew it! She will never talk to you again, so I'm taking over," King said.

"Oh no you're not."

"Do you really want me to play that tape? To those up

there?" He nodded towards the ceiling. O'Neil looked crestfallen. "I didn't think so." King picked his papers up off the table. "Leave it to me. Perhaps she will come round at a later date."

Chapter 32

Tommy had made the phone call the day before and arranged a meet with Maxi and his younger brother Michael. He had brought the disc with him, along with a laptop so he could play the film to them. He didn't know what sort of reaction he would get, but he knew they wouldn't like what they were about to see. Their friendship went back many years; in fact, it was Maxi who had introduced Colin to Tommy and the boys, Stevie and Johnny. And from then on they had been a tight-knit firm for nigh on twenty-five years.

When they were younger they were one of the top firms in London, mainly working in the south of the river, but every now and then, if the prize was big enough, they would spread their wings and come across the water. Between them they had only a couple of lay downs; only Tommy had done a long stretch out of the four of them. Colin was their fixer and he had always spread enough money around to keep them out of prison. Kaye, Tommy's wife, was devastated when Tommy got sent down but she never went without. The others saw to that.

Once he got through the Blackwall Tunnel, Tommy made his way to the Old Ford Road and then headed towards Hackney Road. About halfway down he turned off to the right and found the little trading estate where Maxi had his workshops and offices. He parked up opposite the back door. As he got out of the car he stretched his arms out, trying to relieve his aching back. Then, taking the laptop out of the car, he walked to the outer office door, pressed the entry phone and waited for a reply. Looking around, he noticed the camera pointing down at him. That was new. On hearing the door buzz, he pushed it open and climbed the stairs. He started to think through the reasoning for him coming over to see Maxi. It was simple: Colin was their fixer – the person who knew everyone to go to. The one to find out who was who and what could be done about it. But Colin was dead, and Maxi was the only one Tommy could think of who would have the knowledge and knowhow to help him out of this predicament.

He reached the top of the stairs and spotted another camera staring down at him. He also noticed the office door was different. Instead of the old wooden one with a window in it, he was looking at a metal door. The place was like Fort Knox.

The door opened before he could take hold of the handle. Michael stood before him, smiling. "Hello Tom."

"Michael," he said. They shook hands.

"Maxi's in the loo. Take a seat." Tommy sat down in the chair opposite Maxi's desk. "How's Kaye?" Michael asked.

"She's fine, Mike. As long as she has the kids and her horses, she's happy."

Maxi entered the room. "Tommy, nice to see you. What brings you this side of the water?" He walked over to Tommy and started to shake his hand.

"Tell you the truth, Max, I'm here for a bit of help."

"And how's that?" said Maxi, as he sat down at his desk.

"Well, as you know, Colin and Natasha were murdered."

"Terrible, terrible news, Tom. Colin was one of my oldest friends. Do you know when the funeral will take place?"

"Haven't the foggiest, Max. The Old Bill still have the bodies and they're not ready to release them."

"Any clues as to why they were murdered, and by whom?" Maxi leaned back in his chair, stroking his chin.

"That's why I'm here to see you."

Maxi looked surprised. "How can I help?" he said. He sat up and rested his arms on the desk.

Tommy got up. "I have the killers on film." He placed the computer on Maxi's desk.

"You what?"

"I have everything – and I warn you, you're going to need a strong stomach to watch it." Maxi looked at Michael, who looked just as stunned as he felt. Tommy booted up the computer, took the disc out of its box and placed it in the disc drive. Then he turned the screen towards Maxi. "Michael, you want to come round this side?" He gestured to Maxi's left. Michael walked around the desk and stood behind his brother.

The first image they saw was Colin and Natasha in bed drinking coffee. Then they watched Natasha get up, put on her dressing gown and go out of the room. "I think someone rang the doorbell, but you can't hear it," said Tommy. Seconds later Natasha came back into the room, only she wasn't alone. A man, six foot three or four and wearing a suit, was holding her by her hair. They watched him throw her onto the bed violently. She rolled across the bed onto the floor, her dressing gown hanging off her shoulders, leaving her breasts exposed.

Two more men had followed them into the bedroom. One went to Colin's side of the bed and threatened him with a baseball bat. Colin held out his hands in front of him. They could see the big man in the suit was shouting at him. Colin seemed to be saying "Calm down."

"There's no sound, Tom. What's he bloody saying?"

"Sorry, Max, but there must have been something wrong with their system."

The man in the suit was screaming at the couple, and Colin started to shout back at the suit. "This is when it all goes ape shit," Tommy said. They watched as the first blow caught Colin on the side of his head. He fell back, stunned. By now Natasha was on her knees with a gun in her hand. She shot the man with the baseball bat in the mouth, but the bullet came out the other side of his cheek and into the wall, sending blood and flesh everywhere. He screamed out in pain, then started beating down on Colin, shouting all kinds of obscenities, it looked like.

The suit pulled a gun out of his waistband and shot Natasha four times in the head and body. Colin somehow managed to fight his way up from the bed and was trying to strangle the guy who had been hitting him with the baseball bat.

The third man produced a chainsaw from a holdall and had started it up on the second pull of the cord. Colin didn't see it coming. The bastard placed the chainsaw on his neck and calmly began to sever his head from his shoulders.

Maxi gripped the sides of his chair. "Jesus Christ!"

Michael's fists turned white with rage as he clutched at the edge of the desk. "Max, we have to find these cunts! They're taking us out one by one."

They continued watching the video. Blood sprayed up onto the wall and over the ceiling. Colin's head rolled off his shoulders onto the floor but his hands were still around the second man's throat. His body appeared to be doing a funny dance of its own as it lost control and fell onto the bed.

The suit, who was laughing at Colin's body actions, started to copy them, holding out his hands as if he was strangling someone whilst doing a break dance. Chainsaw joined in while the man with the bat shouted something at them. He didn't seem to find it funny; he was rubbing his neck where Colin's hands had been.

Suit took control and gave the other two some orders. First they picked up Natasha's body and placed it on the bed, sitting upright. Then they placed Colin's decapitated body next to Natasha's. The suit started to laugh again and was pointing, and they realised Colin still had an erection from all the Viagra he had taken that morning.

The suit seemed to be telling baseball man to do something. At first he protested. Then he started laughing. He wrapped Colin's penis in tissues that he took from a box on the bedside cabinet. Then, taking a butterfly knife from his pocket and flipping it open, he pulled on Colin's dick and cut it off in one stroke. He then walked around the bed and went to place it in Natasha's mouth, but the suit stopped him and gave Chainsaw orders to cut off Natasha's head and swap it with Colin's. They looked at each other and started to laugh again; the arseholes seemed to find this hilarious. By the time they were finished, the scene they left behind looked like something out of the Texas Chainsaw Massacre, with blood splattered all over the walls and ceiling.

As Tommy turned off the computer, there was a stunned silence in the room. Maxi broke the tension. "Colin and Natasha's murders will be avenged. These people obviously can't be English. They must be Eastern European or Russian. The kind of violence being used here is very rare and not seen that often. In fact, I find it sickening. But I feel this is something we are going to have to get used to, and we are going to have to fight fire with fire and be just as brutal as them when we find them. I also think they are trying to send us a message. Why, I don't know. But I think the bastards want to take everything and everyone from us."

"Tom," Michael said, "our own brother was attacked right here in this very office, and we have no idea who did it. But you have given us something to work with." He came around the table to Tommy. "Do you mind if we have a copy of this? We have a very good private investigator who may be able to help us out."

"Mike, I don't want this to get into the wrong hands."

"It won't, Tom. I'll just take some images of their faces and show them to him. He is very discreet; he's done a fair bit of work for us in the past."

"If you vouch for him, that's fine by me," Tommy said.

Maxi interrupted. "What are you going to do if we find them for you?"

Tommy thought for a moment. Then he shrugged his shoulders and said, "Kill them. Colin and Natasha didn't deserve to die like that. No one does."

Maxi saw tears in Tommy's eyes. "Lots of things are happening at the moment, Tom. Some I cannot understand, and some I can." He sat back in his chair. "We have become lazy. We've had it cushty for too long. I suppose we could all just walk away. None of us are short of a few bob. But I say fuck that. I'm not ready to give up this life yet. Are you?" Tommy smiled and nodded in agreement. "We're old school, Tom. Personally, I couldn't do violence like that to anyone."

"I fuckin' can," said Michael.

Maxi looked at his younger brother. "But then you always could, Michael." He walked over to a mini fridge and took out a bottle of Scotch. "But we have youngsters who are coming up around us. And these are good boys, boys we can trust. Drink, Tom?"

"Not for me, Max."

"Well I'm having one. I need one after what you just showed me. Mike?" He raised the empty glass.

"Small one for me please, Max."

Maxi poured Scotch into two glasses and added a handful of ice that chinked as it hit the sides. He handed Michael one, then swilled the ice around in his own glass before he took a sip. He smiled at Tommy. "Now leave this to us for now, Tom, and when we hear some news we will let you know."

The End

About the Author

JD Carter lives in Essex, England with his wife, Jacqueline. He moved out of London twenty-one years ago to give his children a better start in life, as he felt the schools were of a much better quality than the inner-city schools he was used to. He has never regretted it.

The Fight Back is the second book in a trilogy of the story of Alex Dicks. JD Carter wishes to say sorry to his readers that it has been so long since the first book in the series, The Party – but please enjoy.